barcode on next page

D0455932

FROM THE
NANCY DREW FILES

THE CASE: Nancy investigates a pattern of sabotage and poaching on an animal research project.

CONTACT: While Ned trails the yellow-bellied marmot, Nancy tracks a criminal conspiracy.

SUSPECTS: Professor Dan Trainey—His project is running out of money, but with the marmots worth $500 each, he may have discovered a way to keep it going.

Jack Billings—The park ranger is Mr. Charm, but while he's flirting with Nancy, she may be flirting with danger.

Gerald and Edith Turkower—They claim to be tourists, but Nancy has uncovered evidence that they're concealing their true identities.

COMPLICATIONS: One of Nancy's top suspects is Professor Trainey. But Ned seems to care more about him—and his pretty daughter—than he does about Nancy and the truth.

Books in The Nancy Drew Files® Series

Available from ARCHWAY Paperbacks

Case 95

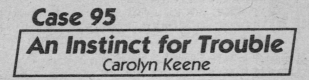

An Instinct for Trouble
Carolyn Keene

AN ARCHWAY PAPERBACK
Published by POCKET BOOKS
New York   London   Toronto   Sydney   Tokyo   Singapore

AN ARCHWAY PAPERBACK *Original*

An Archway Paperback published by
POCKET BOOKS, a division of Simon & Schuster Inc.
1230 Avenue of the Americas, New York, NY 10020

Copyright © 1994 by Simon & Schuster Inc.
Produced by Mega-Books of New York, Inc.

ISBN: 0-671-79487-6

First Archway Paperback printing May 1994

10 9 8 7 6 5 4 3 2 1

NANCY DREW, AN ARCHWAY PAPERBACK and colophon are registered trademarks of Simon & Schuster Inc.

THE NANCY DREW FILES is a trademark of Simon & Schuster Inc.

Cover art by Cliff Miller

Printed in the U.S.A.

IL 6+

Chapter

One

NANCY!" Bess Marvin exclaimed. "Listen —that's Randy Dean's new song, 'Lonely Wilderness.'" She leaned forward and turned up the volume on the car radio, then rolled down her window.

And the trees sway against the blue, blue sky.
But there's danger lurking nearby.
Yes, danger nearby.

"It's like it was meant for us," Bess said when the song ended. "I mean, here we are, with the trees swaying against the blue sky."

Nancy Drew brushed a lock of shoulder-length, reddish blond hair off her face. "Let's hope there's no danger lurking nearby."

"These mountains and forest are gorgeous," Bess said. "And Yellowstone is supposed to be even better—one of the most beautiful places on earth."

It was a cool, crisp Wednesday in early May. That morning Nancy and Bess had flown from their hometown of River Heights to Jackson, Wyoming, where they had rented a car for the drive north to Yellowstone National Park.

"George would love this," Nancy commented as they passed a grove of aspen trees. "Too bad she couldn't come." George Fayne, Bess's cousin, had been forced to pass up the trip because of a long-planned visit to friends in Boston.

"Bet you can't wait to see Ned," Bess said.

Nancy smiled broadly. Her boyfriend was one of a small group of Emerson College students who had been camping in Yellowstone for three weeks, studying the habits of the yellow-bellied marmot, a small, furry mammal common in the park. "I do miss him. I just wish it hadn't taken an emergency to get us together."

"Who was it who got hurt again?" Bess asked.

"A graduate student named Brad Keeler," Nancy replied. "He was badly burned when a propane stove exploded the night before last, and Ned doesn't think it was an accident."

"Because all those marmot traps were stolen, right?" Bess said.

"Right. Over the last couple of weeks about four dozen traps have disappeared. It happened gradually, and no one realized they were missing because they were stored in several different places," Nancy explained. "But Brad finally noticed and was starting to look into it before that stove blew up in his face."

"How awful!" Bess exclaimed. "What was the study group doing with the traps, anyway?"

"They used them to catch the marmots last fall so they could attach transmitters to the animals," Nancy said. "That's how the Emerson people keep track of the marmots' movements."

"Neat," Bess said. "But why would anyone want the traps?"

"Ned thinks someone is planning to trap marmots with them and smuggle them out of the park, which is totally illegal," Nancy answered.

"But he doesn't have any proof, so he called you, since you happen to be not only the love of his life but also an incredible detective," Bess said, grinning.

"Thanks for the compliment, but I'm really worried about this case. This phase of the Emerson study ends on Saturday. Ned says that if any marmots vanish between now and then, the study could be blamed. The third phase of the project scheduled for this summer would be canceled, and all the college's work would go down the drain." Nancy sighed. "Ned's really upset."

"You don't think that someone from the Emerson group could be involved, do you?"

"I'd hate to think it. But we've got to check," Nancy said solemnly as they passed a sign that said South Entrance, Yellowstone National Park.

Tall, slender lodgepole pines lined the road on either side, their tangy scent filling the car. The trees were so thick in some places that it was like driving through a tunnel.

"I can't wait to see the yellow-bellied marmots," Bess said.

Nancy grinned. "Ned said they look like chubby, overgrown chipmunks, only with yellow undersides, which is how they got their name. But most people call them whistling marmots, because they communicate by making high-pitched sounds."

"They sound cute—" Bess began but stopped abruptly.

A herd of brown elk appeared from among the trees on the right.

Nancy stepped on the brake.

Paying no attention to the car, the elk began prancing gracefully across the road.

"Oh, Nancy, look at the babies!" Bess cried.

Nancy chuckled as a handful of little elk wobbled awkwardly in front of the herd.

The herd stopped in a meadow on the left side of the highway. Near the center of the sparse grass where the creatures were grazing, Nancy noticed a cone of gray rock about a foot high. From its center, wisps of white steam curled into the air.

"It's a geyser!" Nancy exclaimed.

Bess's jaw dropped.

"The whole park is covered with them," Nancy said as she started driving again. "Which is why Yellowstone is so special."

"I read the guidebook, too," Bess said teasingly. "The geysers are remnants of volcanoes that erupted around here millions of years ago. But I still can't believe it."

"Just wait until you see Old Faithful. It erupts about every hour and a half. And it will be right outside our window at the hotel," Nancy said.

"That's why I wanted to stay there," Bess replied.

Nancy shook her head and laughed at her friend. "You just didn't want to camp out, even though it would be better if we were closer to the study group."

"Oh, Nan, I can't!" she moaned. "I hate bugs, but even worse I hate sleeping on the cold, bumpy ground."

"Okay, okay," Nancy said. "You convinced me. But you may be passing up the chance to get close to a cute Emerson guy," she warned her friend.

Nancy stepped on the brake at an intersection. A sign pointed right to the Grand Loop Road and left to the inn and visitors center. Before she could turn, a tour bus passed in front of her. She followed it in the direction of the inn.

"It seems a bit early in the season for tour buses," Nancy said.

"It's probably better to get here before the main tourist season starts," Bess replied. "Is Ned meeting us at the hotel?"

"He said he'd try to. But the Emerson group is incredibly busy right now, gearing up for the end of this phase of the study," Nancy explained. "If he's not there when we arrive, we'll head over to the campsite after we check in."

The road grew steeper, and Nancy kept a safe distance between her white rental car and the bus in front. On the far side of the pass, the highway ran beside a gushing river.

"That must be the hotel," Bess said, pointing to the left. "Have you ever seen anything like it in your life?"

Nancy leaned forward and saw a building that was at least seven stories high with a slanted roof and rows of little dormer windows. Its walls were made of huge rough-cut logs stacked one on top of the other.

"It looks like a giant birdhouse," Nancy said delightedly as she turned onto the road that led to the inn and followed it to the front of the building. Then, remembering that Ned might be waiting for her inside, she hastily stopped the car, turned off the ignition, and jumped out.

"Go on ahead, Nancy," Bess urged with a knowing smile. "I'll find someone to help me with the bags. Then I'll park the car in the lot over there," she said, pointing.

Gratefully, Nancy tossed Bess the car keys, mounted the wooden stairs, and entered the lobby.

The center of the building was an atrium that rose all the way to the roof. Along two sides were level after level of balconies. A huge fireplace of gigantic lava stones dominated the big space. Half a dozen guests sat near the fire in old-fashioned rocking chairs. Another row of rockers faced tall windows overlooking several geysers. A few people were seated there, enjoying the view. But no Ned. Nancy choked back her disappointment.

Just then she saw Bess enter the lobby, followed by a bellhop pulling a trolley with Bess's two suitcases and Nancy's small carry-on bag.

"Where's Ned?" she asked when Nancy reached her side.

Nancy shook her head. "At the campsite, I guess. I'd like to drive over and take a look."

"Okay, go ahead," Bess said, handing the car keys back to her friend. "I'll check us in and start unpacking."

Nancy walked to the parking lot briskly. The sun shone brightly, but the air was chilly. She spotted the car, dashed over, and got in. After glancing at the map Ned had faxed her, she started the engine and headed north for about fifteen miles.

At Madison Junction, where there was a ranger station, general store, and campground, she turned right. She watched carefully until she spotted a dirt road leading off to the left, then bumped along it for about a quarter of a mile to the campsite.

The Emerson College research group was camping at the foot of a hill in a clearing partly ringed by lodgepole pines. Nancy parked next to a Jeep and walked quickly up the path toward the little cluster of woodland green tents. When she reached the fire pit at its center, she found the campsite deserted.

Several logs had been pulled around the fire pit to serve as benches. Not far away was the kitchen tent, with sides made of mosquito netting and tables lined with pots, pans, and food.

A narrow trail snaked along the edge of the camp and then continued up the hill. Near the foot of the hill, and about a hundred yards from the campsite, was a very small, wooden cabin. Nancy went over to inspect it.

There was a heavy padlock on the door and only one tiny window, through which she could see a generator and computer. Next to the door, on the outside of the cabin, was a makeshift bulletin board. Nancy studied the work assignment chart posted there. It was divided into categories such as Computer Data Collection, Transmitter Checking, and Observation—Feeding Stations 1 through 4.

Nancy saw that Ned was assigned to watch

feeding station 3 from two-thirty to five that afternoon. Where was he now, though? she wondered. It was just about two.

She strolled back toward the tents. The canvas flap that served as a door on the nearest one was tied back. She glanced inside and saw a camera bag that reminded her of Ned's, then started to raise the mosquito netting and go inside.

"Stop right there!" she heard someone shout behind her.

Nancy spun around and saw two men in dark green coveralls running toward her. The taller one, who had piercing black eyes and black stubble for a beard, reached her first. He grabbed her by the arm and yanked her away from the tent.

"Hey," Nancy protested, struggling to free herself from his grip. "I wasn't doing anything wrong."

Just then the second man reached her. He was built like a short redwood and had the ruddy complexion of someone who spent a lot of time outdoors.

"Yeah, sure," the tall man said, twisting Nancy's arm behind her.

Nancy had to bite her lip to keep from crying out.

"Looks like we caught ourselves a thief," the short, burly guy said, taking a step toward her. An ugly grin contorted his face. "And we know just what to do with her. Right, Richard?"

"Right," his buddy replied.

Chapter

Two

COME ON, YOU," Richard growled. He wheeled Nancy around and started pulling her toward the fire pit.

"Get your hands off me!" Nancy said, furious.

"Not a chance," he replied, tightening his grip. "Should we take her to the truck, Piker?"

"Yeah," the other man replied, giving Nancy a shove.

Nancy swung her leg out and brought it up, slamming her knee into Richard's stomach.

He bent over, giving her the chance to pull away. She was just taking off when she heard a familiar voice call her name.

She whirled around to see Ned hurrying

down the path toward her. "Am I ever glad to see you!" she said with relief.

Ned glanced at the two grim-faced men and put his arm around Nancy. "What's going on here?"

"These guys accused me of being a thief," Nancy told him.

"What?" Ned was incredulous. "This is my girlfriend."

Richard shrugged. "If you say so, but she was nosing around camp. Right, Piker?"

"Right," Piker said. "We were just looking out for your group," he told Ned. "We heard there'd been some trouble around here."

"Well, thanks," Ned replied. "But like I said, Nancy's my girlfriend."

Nancy watched Piker nervously shift his weight. At last he nodded and said, "Well, okay. Let's get back to work, Richard." With that, the two men headed off.

"That's quite a welcoming committee," Nancy said.

Before she could say anything else, Ned swept her into his arms. "Hello there," he said as he lifted her chin with two fingers. The kiss that followed left her breathless. "How's that for a welcome?"

"Mmm, much better." Nancy sighed and

took in his handsome, square-jawed face and sparkling brown eyes.

Ned led Nancy to one of the logs near the fire pit, and the two of them sat down.

"Who were those guys, anyway?" she asked.

"Park maintenance men," Ned replied. "They're building a walkway near here. It goes to an old cabin near Princess Geyser. What made them think you were a thief?"

"Well," Nancy said, "I was peeking inside a tent, wondering if it was yours, when they grabbed me. I guess I *did* look a little suspicious."

"Even so," Ned growled, "they had no right to treat you badly." He took her hand. "Listen, Nan, I'm really sorry I couldn't meet you at the hotel. The fact is, we have a major crisis. You know, we've tagged hundreds of marmots so we can track them. Well, part of my job is to make sure the receiver is picking up their signals and sending them to the computer so they're recorded properly."

Nancy nodded.

"This morning," he said slowly, "the computer printout showed no trace of almost fifty whistling marmots. At first, I thought we had a problem with the receiver or with the computer, but everything checked out okay. We went

14

out to check the marmot colonies a few hours ago, and it was obvious that some were missing. There's only one logical explanation. Someone is stealing them!"

"That's terrible," Nancy said. "Do you have any idea when it could have happened?"

"We observe the marmots twice a day at four feeding stations," he explained, pacing now. "So it had to have happened after the second observation yesterday—probably during the night."

Nancy shook her head. "It's hard to believe that people would kill such cute little animals for their fur," she said disgustedly.

Ned stopped pacing. "It's not the fur they want," he replied. "They want the marmots for pets."

"That's no excuse for taking them out of their natural habitat," Nancy said. "Have you reported this to the park service?"

"Sure," Ned replied. "But without more evidence the park service can't launch a full-scale investigation. They just don't have the financial resources to act on our suspicions."

"That's awful," Nancy said.

"My sentiments exactly," Ned agreed. "Of course, the park service did assign a really good ranger named Jack Billings to our project. But his job is to help us, not track down poachers."

"Just what is it you're doing in this project?" Nancy asked, stretching her legs out. "I know you're studying marmots. Are they endangered?"

"No, but their cousins, the Vancouver Island marmots, are," he said. "Professor Trainey's plan is to research the whistling marmots in Yellowstone so we can figure out what conditions marmots best thrive in. The information we gather here will be used by biologists to breed Vancouver Island marmots in captivity."

"That's wonderful," Nancy said.

Ned nodded. "From the first moment I heard Professor Trainey talk about the study, I knew I wanted to help. He even got a federal grant to buy a state-of-the-art tracking system."

Nancy cocked her head curiously.

"Imagine a transmitter no bigger than a dime that tells us not only where the animal is," Ned went on, "but its body temperature, blood pressure, eating and sleeping cycles— it's just amazing!"

"And amazingly expensive, I bet," Nancy commented.

Ned nodded his agreement and pulled her to

her feet. "Come on, I'll show you around. First stop is our command post."

He led Nancy across the campsite to the tiny cabin she had stopped at earlier. He pulled a key ring from his jeans pocket, undid the padlock, pushed open the door, and switched on the light that dangled from the ceiling. Nancy followed him inside.

Along one wall was a plank table that held the computer and printer. A small file cabinet in the corner was heaped high with printouts.

"The device that receives the radio signals from the transmitters is outside," Ned explained.

Nancy pointed to a door at the other side of the room and asked, "Where does that go?"

"To the supply room," Ned replied. "That's what we call it, but it's really just a glorified closet. Still, it's big enough to hold traps, sacks of food pellets, and other equipment."

"Is that where the traps were stolen from?" Nancy said.

"Some of them," Ned answered. "But we've got four marmot observation stations, and we keep traps in the huts there, too." Ned leaned against the worktable. "It makes me sick to think that the poachers are using our equipment to steal marmots!"

Nancy returned to the door and studied

the padlock. The shiny brass lock was unscratched. "Who has keys to this cabin?" she asked.

"Just the professor and Brad," Ned replied. "These are the professor's keys I have. He gave them to me. We were at observation station two, but he wanted me to come back to check the computer to see if any signals from the missing marmots had shown up."

"Could I see one of the traps?" Nancy asked.

Ned went through the other door and returned with a wire cage with open doors at each end.

"We put food inside," Ned explained. "When a marmot steps in to get it, its weight triggers a spring that closes the doors."

Ned picked up a small disk attached to a plastic collar. "Then we attach a transmitter to the animal's neck."

Nancy studied the collar. "And the marmots don't mind?"

"Usually not," Ned said with a smile. "Now and then we have to tranquilize one." He indicated a small hypodermic syringe on a shelf.

Nancy shuddered.

"It doesn't hurt," he insisted. "And anyway, we don't have to do it very often. Most of the marmots, especially those under two years old, are really cooperative."

"What happens after the collar is on?" she asked.

"Each transmitter has its own identifying signal," Ned told her. "All of them are picked up on our receiver and automatically fed into the computer. Then, two times a day, we download the file and chart the movements of the animals we're tracking. Since Brad's accident, that's been my job."

"How's Brad doing?" Nancy asked.

"Better," Ned said. "But they've kept him pretty heavily sedated. No one's been able to see him."

"Where did he get hurt?" Nancy queried.

"Up the hill in the hut at observation post one," Ned replied.

"I'd like to see it," Nancy said.

Ned led Nancy to the trail that wound up the hill. At the top of the slope, Ned halted. "Well," he said with a sweep of his hand, "this is it. We have three other feeding stations, but this is the most important one."

Nancy looked around. They were on level ground now. A circular area about the size of a football field had been fenced off with chicken wire.

"This is a marmot community, and that's one of their burrows," Ned explained, pointing to a raised mound on the far side of the chicken wire.

Inside the enclosure Nancy noticed a slim girl about her own age leaning down to a burrow. She was wearing a checked shirt, straight-legged jeans, and suede boots. Her long black hair was pulled back into a ponytail, and she had pale blue eyes and an oval face with a pronounced widow's peak. When she saw Nancy and Ned, she came over to greet them.

"Hi, Jennifer, this is Nancy Drew," Ned said casually. "Nancy, meet Jennifer Trainey."

"Hi, Jennifer," Nancy said. "Trainey—are you related to the professor?"

"He's my dad," Jennifer said quickly, then added with a slight smile, "Ned didn't tell me he was expecting company."

Nancy was about to respond when she noticed a flicker of movement from inside the enclosure. She saw a small head peering out of one of the burrows. As she watched, delighted, a marmot emerged. Another was close behind. They were reddish brown with yellow abdomens and black rings near their bushy tails.

"Meet Click and Clack, our most sociable specimens," Jennifer said.

"They're adorable." Nancy glanced at Jennifer. "You must have been in on this project from the very beginning."

Jennifer laughed. "Since *before* the very beginning," she replied.

The two marmots finished eating. One sat up on its hind legs. The furry creature had a wide head with short, rounded ears, large eyes, and a black button nose. It cocked its head sideways as if to ask Nancy what she was doing there and then began grooming itself.

"Wait until Bess sees these. She'll go crazy," Nancy said. "It looks like they'd be really fun to work with."

"Oh, they are!" Jennifer exclaimed. "Right now I'm monitoring the day care center."

"Day care center?" Nancy echoed.

"While the parents are out foraging for food, the older members of the community stay in the entrances to the burrows, making sure the babies are safe," Jennifer explained. "If they sense danger, they give a shrill ear-piercing whistle."

"Did many marmots disappear from this feeding station?" Nancy asked.

Jennifer raised her eyebrows.

"It's okay," Ned said quickly. "I told Nancy about what happened. She can be trusted—she's my girlfriend."

"Oh," Jennifer said smoothly. "How long are you here for?"

"A few days," Nancy replied.

"Great," Jennifer said, though Nancy doubted her sincerity. "Well, I'd better get back to work," she went on without answering Nancy's question. "See you later."

As Jennifer walked away, Nancy turned to Ned. "She's incredibly pretty," she said.

Ned reddened and shrugged, then led Nancy toward a small hut. As they approached it, Nancy noticed a metal box on top of a pole. She saw another one just like it about fifty yards farther along the fence. "What are those things?" she asked.

"Time-lapse cameras," Ned replied. "They're set to take exposures every fifteen minutes. They even record the date and time at the bottom of each negative."

"Incredible," Nancy said, then pointed to the hut. "Is that where Brad was hurt?"

"Yeah," Ned replied. "We keep a few snacks and drinks in there. Apparently, Brad was heating water for coffee, when *boom!* I heard the explosion and ran up the hill. Brad was lying across the doorstep, unconscious."

Nancy shook her head sympathetically. "The force of the explosion must have blown him out the door. He's lucky he wasn't killed."

Inside the hut were two chairs and a folding table covered with computer printouts and camera gear. Several bags of food pellets and a stack of traps lined the far wall. Above it was a shelf with a canister of sugar, instant coffee, and tea bags.

Nancy pointed to a blackened object in the corner of the room. "Is that the stove that blew up?"

Ned nodded, and she went over to it. The stove consisted of one burner attached by a copper tube to a canister of propane. Nancy checked the propane tank. The fitting between it and the tubing was tight, but when she traced a path up the tubing to the nut that connected it to the burner, she let out a gasp.

"Find something?" Ned asked.

Nancy held the tubing and the bolt up to the light. "Look at this," she said. "See those scratch marks? Someone's tampered with the nut."

Ned's eyes narrowed. "That means when Brad turned on the stove, propane started escaping."

"Exactly," Nancy agreed. "And when he lit the match, there was an explosion."

Ned straighted up. "So it wasn't an accident. Someone deliberately tried to hurt Brad!"

Chapter
Three

O<small>R KILL HIM</small>," Nancy added as she detached the tube and put it in the pocket of her jacket. "This is our first piece of evidence."

From the doorway, someone spoke up. "What's going on here?"

Nancy turned and saw a lanky man of about fifty, whose black hair was sprinkled with gray at the temples. He had a deeply tanned face and a wide, unsmiling mouth. A tall, dark, good-looking guy in a ranger uniform and a young woman clad in blue jeans and a purple Emerson College sweatshirt stood just behind him.

Ned moved toward the group. "I was just showing my friend Nancy around. Professor

Trainey, this is Nancy Drew." He gestured to the two people behind Trainey and added, "That's Jack Billings, a park ranger, and Alicia Nivel, from Emerson."

"Hi. You're Ned's girlfriend from River Heights, aren't you?" A brief smile flashed across Alicia's face. "He talks about you a lot."

For a minute no one said anything. Then the professor turned to Ned. "Did anything new turn up on the computer?" he asked.

Ned ran his hand back through his hair nervously. "Umm—I didn't get a chance to look. Nancy showed up just when I got to the command post," he explained.

"I see," Trainey replied. He crossed his arms at his waist and stared at Ned. "We've got fifty marmots missing, final observations to make before we leave on Saturday, at least a day of packing ahead of us—and you've invited a visitor here. I must say, your timing surprises me."

Ned swallowed. "But, sir, Nancy is—"

Trainey held up his hand. "I need you down at camp in ten minutes to draft a plot of today's readings." He turned and headed down the path.

Alicia gave Nancy an apologetic smile and said, "You'll have to forgive us. We're all pretty tense these days, what with the marmots missing and the grant extension hanging in the balance."

The ranger patted her on the back and said, "Don't worry, Alicia. You'll make it."

"Thanks, Jack," Alicia replied.

Ned shook his head despondently. "I just wish Trainey had given me a chance to explain why I invited Nancy. She's a well-known detective and is going to track down the poachers."

Nancy would have preferred to keep her role a secret for a little while longer. Oh, well, too late now, she thought.

Jack gave Nancy a big smile. "A private eye," he said. "Well, I'll be. And a pretty one, too."

Nancy tried to keep from blushing, but it was no use. She thought that Jack was amazingly handsome—rugged and intelligent looking, too. She turned to Alicia and asked, "What did you mean about the grant extension?"

"Our study is being paid for by a federal grant," Alicia said. "But there were cost overruns, so Professor Trainey applied for an extension, but in the meantime he's been paying some of the expenses out of his own pocket."

Nancy whistled. "That's pretty daring of him," she said. "Is he wealthy?"

"I doubt it," Ned said. "He lives in a small cottage off campus and drives a beat-up truck. His work is about the only thing that seems to matter to him."

Nancy turned to Jack. "I met a couple of park maintenance men today named Richard and Piker. Do you know them?"

Jack hitched his thumbs in his belt and said, "Yes, I do. Why?"

"They weren't exactly friendly when I met them at the campsite a little while ago," Nancy replied.

Jack gazed at Nancy. "I'm sorry if they gave you a hard time. I told them about what happened to Brad and asked them to be on the lookout for trouble. Actually, Piker and Richard are really good guys," Jack went on. "They're just better at building walkways than relating to the public."

"Oh," Nancy said, keeping her doubts to herself. "Ned told me about Brad's accident. That was the day before yesterday at about eight in the evening, right?"

"Seven fifty-three, to be exact," Ned said.

Nancy flashed him a grateful smile and continued. "Were either of you around when it happened?"

Jack gave a vigorous shake of his head. "Not me. I was at the ranger station, giving a talk on the mammals of Yellowstone. It started at seven."

"That's right," Alicia said. "Jennifer and I were there. The slides were terrific!"

"Did either of you happen to use the stove that afternoon?" Nancy asked, her eyes casually moving from Jack to Alicia and back.

Alicia frowned in concentration. "I think I did. When I came up to change the film in the cameras, I made some hot chocolate."

"What time was that?" Nancy pressed.

"Six-thirty," Alicia replied. "I left about ten minutes later to go to the lecture. I made it just in time."

"I remember you huffing and puffing as you ran into the room," Jack said with a grin. "But speaking of time, Trainey told us to meet him in ten minutes."

"And me in the doghouse already!" Ned exclaimed. "Come on, Nancy."

Nancy and Ned jogged down the path to the campsite with Alicia and Jack close behind them. When they reached the parking area, Ned gave Nancy a quick kiss, then dashed off.

Nancy drove away, thinking about the investigation. If Alicia's recollection was correct, the propane stove was working at six-thirty on the day of the accident. But by seven fifty-three, it had been sabotaged. If she could place someone at the observation hut during that time period, it would go a long way toward breaking the case.

As she drove up to the hotel, she saw Bess standing on the porch, peering anxiously at the road. The moment she spotted Nancy, she started waving wildly. Nancy parked and ran over to her.

"What is it, Bess?" she demanded. "What's wrong?"

"Nothing's wrong," Bess replied. "I think I just solved the whole case!"

"What do you mean?" Nancy sank down onto a porch swing.

Bess dropped down next to Nancy and handed her a piece of paper. "Just look at this," she said.

Nancy's eyes widened when she read the title: "Hot New Pet Craze—Whistling Marmots." The sheet had been photocopied from a magazine. In the article the words native to Yellowstone were highlighted in orange. Nancy's heart began to race. "Where did you get this?"

"I was sitting in the lobby," Bess explained, "when a rich-looking couple came in and stopped near me. As they moved away, I noticed a piece of paper on the floor, so I picked it up."

"Hmm." Nancy scanned the page and read out loud. "'Rock star Randy Dean's fondness for collecting marmots has made the creature a sought-after pet among the rich and famous. According to one U.S. wildlife specialist, some people are willing to pay as much as five hundred dollars for one of these animals.'"

"Randy keeps a bunch of marmots on his California estate," Bess said. "According to the article, one of them escaped. A neighbor found it in her kitchen, munching its way through a box of cereal. The story made the newspapers, and ever since then people have wanted marmots."

"That's very interesting," Nancy said slowly. "I guess we should find out the couple's names and where they come from."

Bess grinned proudly. "They're Gerald and Edith Turkower, and they're from—just guess —Bel Air, California."

Nancy stared. "How do you know?"

"Simple," Bess said smugly. "While they were registering, I checked their luggage tags."

"Good work," Nancy told her friend. "Tell you what," she added, "as a reward, I'll treat you to a cup of tea and a snack. I'll also fill you in on what I've learned so far."

The dining room had log walls and wooden ceiling beams. As they sat down at a table near the windows, Bess leaned forward and whispered, "Two tables to your left—those are the Turkowers."

Nancy casually glanced in their direction as the waitress arrived to take her order.

Then, just as their pie and tea arrived, a bellhop walked through the dining room, saying, "Nancy Drew, telephone call for Nancy Drew."

Nancy waved to him and identified herself.

"It sounds like an emergency," he told her, pulling a cordless phone from a holster on his belt.

"Hello? Yes?" Nancy said.

"Nancy, thank goodness I got you," a breathless voice said. "It's Alicia Nivel. You've got to come at once. Ned's been hurt!"

Chapter

Four

Nancy CLUTCHED the phone so tightly that her knuckles turned white. "What happened?"

"We don't know," Alicia replied. "We found him on the floor at the command post unconscious. He must have fallen and hit his head on something. When he came to, he asked us to call you right away, so I drove down to the general store at Madison Junction."

"I'll be there as soon as possible." Nancy switched off the phone and sprang up from her seat. "Ned's been hurt," she told Bess. "I have to go to him right away."

"I'll go, too." Bess waved for the waitress and paid the check while Nancy went on ahead to get the car.

The fifteen miles to the campsite seemed to

take forever. When Nancy turned in to the parking area, she flung the door open in one movement, then dashed up to camp and straight to the tiny cabin. Bess followed. Inside, Nancy saw Jack, Jennifer, and Alicia clustered around Ned with an open first-aid kit on the floor nearby. Ned was sitting propped up against the wall, holding his head in his hands.

"Ned!" Nancy cried as she rushed in and knelt beside him. "Are you all right?"

"I feel a lot better now that you're here."

Jennifer reluctantly moved aside so Nancy could look at the back of Ned's head. There was a huge bump and dried blood on it. "What happened?" she asked.

Ned shifted, and as he did, Nancy noticed something gleaming on the floor behind him. She picked it up and tucked it into her pocket.

"Let me think. I was on my way over to the command post. The door was ajar, and it's supposed to be kept shut because there's a lot of valuable hardware in here. So I decided to make sure everything was okay. I got inside, and the next thing I knew, I was lying here with this lump on my head and the mother of all headaches. Somebody must have hit me."

Just then Bess arrived. "Ned," she gasped, "are you okay?"

33

"Hi, Bess," he answered, trying his best to sound normal. "Guys, this is Bess Marvin."

Jennifer and Alicia nodded to Bess. Jack glanced at her, smiled broadly, and held out his hand to shake hers. "Hello there, I'm Jack Billings. Boy, does Ned Nickerson have some great-looking friends."

Bess blushed but said nothing.

Nancy got to her feet. "Someone obviously wanted something. Is all the equipment still here?"

Alicia had been studying the computer table. "It doesn't look as if anything was taken."

Nancy crossed to the supply room. Everything looked much as it had when she had seen it a couple of hours earlier. Then she noticed the hypodermic syringe and several vials of tranquilizer were missing.

"Did anyone take a syringe and some tranquilizer vials out of here?" Nancy asked over her shoulder.

Alicia stepped inside and checked the shelf. "Oh—they *are* missing. But who would have taken them?"

Nancy's thoughts raced. First the group had discovered fifty marmots missing, and now someone seemed to have stolen tranquilizers that could sedate more marmots. Was someone planning to tranquilize the fifty stolen creatures so they could be quietly shipped out of the park?

Before she could ask more questions, Nancy saw Professor Trainey at the doorway.

"Now what?" he demanded, slightly out of breath. "Can't I leave this project for five minutes without—" His voice faded as he noticed Ned on the floor.

"Someone hit Ned over the head," Jennifer told her father. "And tranquilizers are missing from the supply room."

Trainey's eyes widened as he knelt beside Ned. "We've got to get you up to the hospital in Gardiner as soon as we can." He glanced around the room, clearly upset. "Can someone drive him there? We can't take chances—not with a head injury."

"I'll go," Nancy quickly offered. "Where is it?"

"Gardiner is just over the state line in Montana, right outside the north entrance of the park. I'll ride along and show you the way," Jack offered. "Just give me a couple of minutes to clear it with headquarters."

Nancy remembered the object she had stashed in her pocket. She slipped it out unobtrusively. It was a Phi Beta Kappa key. Turning it over, she saw the initials D.T. engraved on the back. Dan Trainey.

She leaned down to pat Ned's shoulder, then crossed the room.

"Professor?" she said quietly. "May I speak to you privately for a moment?"

Frowning, Trainey followed her outside.

"If you're concerned about Ned's care, don't be," he began.

"It's not that," Nancy replied. She showed him the gold medallion. "I found this just now under Ned. It's yours, isn't it?"

Trainey took the key from her palm and examined it. "Yes," he said. "I noticed I'd lost it a few days ago. Thanks."

"How do you suppose it came to be lying under Ned—now?" Nancy asked.

Trainey flushed. "What are you implying?"

"Professor Trainey," Nancy said, "I'm a detective. Something strange is going on here. Ned asked me to help find out what it is."

"Now, look here," Trainey said impatiently. "I have a research assistant in the hospital, another of my students on the way there, fifty marmots missing, and a crucial deadline coming up in a couple of days. The last thing I need is an amateur detective in my hair. Do I make myself clear?"

Nancy remained calm. "Do you realize," she asked, "that someone from your group could be behind all the trouble?"

Trainey's eyes narrowed. "What do you mean?

Knowing she finally had his full attention, Nancy continued. "As I understand it, each marmot's transmitter has its own distinctive code, right?

"Yes, of course," Trainey replied, his voice ominously low.

"So someone could use the computer to pin down an animal's location at any given moment?" she pressed.

"That's what the equipment is designed to do—if you know the codes," Trainey replied.

Nancy fixed her eyes on the professor's face. "And who knows them?"

Trainey shrugged. "Everyone here, I suppose. The list is in the computer. . . ." The professor's voice trailed off as he realized the significance of what he had just said.

"It all points to an inside job, professor," Nancy said quietly.

Trainey scowled. "Look, Ms. Drew, are you suspecting me of jeopardizing my project? That's insulting and crazy."

"I'm not saying—" Nancy began.

The professor interrupted her. "I don't have time for this. Why don't you go sightseeing or something?" he barked, then stalked away.

As Nancy returned to the shed, she thought

that it was unlikely the professor would jeopardize his own project, but until she could prove otherwise, he had to be a suspect.

When she got back to the command post, Ned was sitting up near the computer. Nancy was glad to see that his color was better. "Can you walk?" she asked him.

He smiled and assured her that he could.

"All right, we can go," Jack said from the doorway. As they walked across the campground to the parking area, he moved to Bess's side. "Are you coming to the hospital, too?"

Bess nodded, and Nancy noticed the interest in her friend's blue eyes.

"Good," Jack continued, opening the door for Ned and then the back door of the car for Bess. He slipped in next to her.

As they started off in the direction of the north entrance, Ned asked, "What were you talking to the professor about?"

"The problems the study is having," Nancy replied, being deliberately vague. "He seemed tense."

"He has a right to be," Ned said. "His reputation is riding on the success of this project."

For the rest of the trip, Nancy concentrated on her driving while Jack pointed out landmarks. Ned leaned back in his seat with his eyes closed.

At the hospital the group easily found the emergency room. After Ned and Nancy spoke with the nurse there, an orderly led Ned into an examining room, explaining to Nancy that only the patient was allowed inside. The rest of the group found seats in the waiting room.

"I am totally starved," Bess announced. "It's dinnertime."

"There are some vending machines downstairs," Jack said.

"Is this the hospital Brad is in?" Nancy asked after Bess borrowed some quarters and headed for the elevator.

"Yes," Jack replied.

"I wonder if he's allowed visitors yet."

"I don't know," Jack said. "We can ask. I hope he isn't badly scarred. Burns can be pretty awful."

As he spoke, he rubbed a reddish scar on the back of his left hand. "So, tell me about you and Ned. You seem to know each other pretty well," he continued.

Nancy nodded. "We've been going together for a long time."

"Too bad," Jack said with a charming smile. "If Ned weren't such a nice guy, I'd ask you to the square dance tomorrow night at the Old Faithful Inn."

"That's where we're staying," Nancy remarked.

"Then you've got no excuse for missing it," he said, casually draping an arm across the back of Nancy's chair.

"Are you sure I can't tempt you to go with me?" Jack asked teasingly.

Nancy felt flattered but shook her head. "I have a feeling Ned wouldn't like that too much," she answered lightly. "But maybe I'll see you there."

Jack gave a mock sigh of disappointment. "Too bad. Ned's a lucky guy."

From the doorway Ned said, "I sure am. The doctor says I'll be fine. No concussion or anything—but I had to have a few stitches." He gestured to the bandage wrapped all the way around his head. It gave him a roguish look.

Just then Bess came rushing up. "Are they done with you already?" she asked. "Can we go now?"

"I'd like to meet Brad," Nancy replied. "If they'll let us in to see him."

"Good idea," Ned said.

They asked for Brad's room number at the front desk, then filed into the elevator. At the nurse's station they learned that he was conscious and able to receive visitors. A couple of minutes later the group piled into Brad's room. His face and arms were heavily bandaged, but his eyes lit up when he saw them.

"Ned, Jack!" he said, and grinned. "It's great to see you!" He turned his gaze to Nancy and Bess.

"This is my girlfriend, Nancy Drew, and her friend Bess Marvin," Ned explained.

"Nice to meet you," Brad said. Then he noticed Ned's bandage. "Hey, guy, what happened?"

Ned told him.

"We are some hard luck bunch," Brad said. "First me, and now you."

"Don't forget that marmot that nipped me on the nose last week," Jack interjected with a laugh.

"That's right," Brad replied. "Maybe you should watch your step if you're going to hang around with us, Nancy."

Ned filled Brad in about the missing marmots. "After the stove exploded I asked Nancy to come out to look into it. She's a detective, and if anyone can figure out who's causing all the trouble, she can."

"Tell me about your accident, Brad," Nancy began.

"There's not much to tell. The first thing I did when I went on duty was make a cup of coffee."

"Of course," Ned said, grinning. "He's a caffeine addict."

Brad smiled back, then continued. "When I went to light the stove, there was a whoosh, and then flames were everywhere. The next thing I knew, I woke up here."

"How terrible!" Bess exclaimed.

Brad's face hardened. "Yeah, well, I'm not so sure it was an accident. I saw someone sneaking out of the hut as I walked up the path."

Nancy leaned forward eagerly. "Could you tell who it was?"

Brad stared up at the ceiling for a long time. Finally he said, "I hate to say it, but it looked an awful lot like Dan Trainey."

Chapter

Five

N₀ WAY," Ned said. "How could you even think that the professor had anything to do with it?"

Brad shook his head. "All I can tell you is that whoever it was was wearing a dark green hat and a green coat like the professor's. And considering the way he ran behind the hut, I'd say he didn't want to be seen."

"Well, it wasn't Professor Trainey," Ned insisted. "And that's that."

Reluctantly, Nancy told them about finding the professor's Phi Beta Kappa key.

Ned scowled. "There's bound to be an explanation. Did you ask him about it?"

"Yes," Nancy told him. "He said he noticed he lost it a few days ago."

"Well, there you are," Ned concluded. "It was probably on the floor all this time."

Nancy glanced at Ned, who looked upset. She decided to drop the subject for a while. Turning back to Brad, she asked, "Can you think of any reason why anyone would want to hurt you?"

"When I noticed that the traps were missing, the others divided up my chores so I could look into it. Maybe my investigation bothered somebody," Brad suggested.

Nancy nodded thoughtfully. "Did you discover anything?"

Before Brad could answer, a nurse came bustling in. Nancy could almost hear the starch rustling in her white uniform.

"Sorry, folks. Visiting hours are over." She took Brad's wrist between her fingers and checked her watch.

The group said their goodbyes. As they left, Nancy decided to return the next day to question Brad further.

On the way back, Ned sat silently beside Nancy. She could tell he was thinking about the professor. Jack and Bess kept up a steady stream of conversation in the backseat, and Nancy was glad of it.

"I have an idea," Jack said as Nancy turned onto the dirt road leading to the campsite.

"There's a new little café with disco music in West Yellowstone. I know Ned has to rest this evening, but we could go dancing."

"That sounds great," Bess replied.

"Thanks, but I'll pass," Nancy said. "You guys go without me."

"Sure you don't mind?" Bess asked.

Nancy shook her head.

When she parked the car, Jack climbed out, then put his head in through the window. "I'll come by the hotel around eight, okay?" he said to Bess. "If you change your mind, you can still join us," he added to Nancy.

"Oh, wait," Bess called, getting out and walking up the path after Jack. "What kind of place is this? I need to know what to wear."

Jack laughed and put his arm around Bess's shoulders. The two of them bent their heads together and launched into an animated conversation.

Nancy looked over at Ned. He was sitting very stiffly, staring straight ahead. "Are you feeling all right?" she asked.

"I'm fine," he said in a tense voice. But then he added, "There's no way Dan Trainey tampered with that stove, Nancy."

Nancy was silent, and Ned guessed the reason. "You're not listening to me, are you?"

"I'm listening," Nancy said. "But I have to

check him out, and what Brad said makes him a suspect." When Ned didn't respond, she continued. "Of course I'm investigating everyone."

Nancy hoped for a goodbye kiss, but Ned simply opened the door and walked away. Without a word, he passed Bess as she returned to the car.

"Brrr!" Bess said, climbing into the passenger seat. "Did you and Ned just have a fight?"

Nancy swallowed back tears but didn't feel like talking on the drive back to the hotel. Bess was quiet, too, until they turned in to the parking lot. Then she said, "Let's go watch Old Faithful."

Nancy would have preferred to lie down with a book, but she laughed and said, "Okay, Old Faithful it is!"

The girls went through the lobby and followed a path to the geyser.

"Come on," Bess urged. "I see two spots on that bench over there. We'd better grab them."

They sat down and studied the center of attention, a four-foot-high cone that looked like a shrunken volcano. Small puffs of white steam trailed lazily upward from it.

Suddenly there was a rumbling sound as if a truck were passing. Water bubbled up over the surface of the cone and shot at least a hundred feet into the air. Finally, after two or three minutes, the column of water slowly sank and then vanished.

"Wow!" Bess exclaimed.

Nancy just smiled.

Touching her arm, Bess said in an undertone, "Look over there. See the guy with all the camera equipment? That's Turkower."

Nancy saw a couple in their forties. The man was tall, with salt-and-pepper hair and a mustache. He had two expensive-looking cameras around his neck and a leather camera bag over one shoulder. Mrs. Turkower could have just stepped out of a beauty salon.

"Come on, Bess," Nancy urged. "I want to meet them."

The two girls strolled around the geyser and stopped next to the Turkowers. Nancy took the photocopied article about the marmots out of her pocket.

"Excuse me," she said politely. "Did you drop this? I looked for you earlier, but you'd already gone upstairs."

"So that's where it went," the woman said with a tittering laugh. As she accepted the sheet of paper she added, "Thanks for returning it."

"I'm Nancy Drew and this is my friend Bess Marvin."

"Gerald and Edith Turkower here," the man replied. "Smile!" he said suddenly. Before Nancy and Bess could react, he raised the camera and took three quick shots of them.

"I wasn't ready!" Bess protested.

"Gerald, really!" Edith admonished. "He's such a camera nut."

"I couldn't help looking at that article," Nancy said casually. "Those whistling marmots are so cute! Wouldn't it be fun to have one as a pet?"

"Oh, yes," Edith replied. "I know a woman back home who has three of them."

"Edith likes owning unusual things," Gerald said, shooting a keen glance at Nancy.

"I know there are lots of them here in Yellowstone. But isn't it illegal to take animals out of a national park?" Nancy asked, sounding naive.

Gerald nodded. "Sure." Then he smiled knowingly. "But there are ways around that."

Nancy's heartbeat quickened. Did this couple want to buy a marmot? Or were they somehow involved in the poaching scheme? She decided to dangle a little bait and see if one of them took it. "I might consider it, but only if I was sure I wouldn't get into any trouble."

"Nobody likes trouble," Gerald said. To Nancy's disappointment, he didn't say more before they wandered off.

"What do you think, Nan?" Bess asked. "Could they be stealing the marmots?"

Nancy frowned. "They seem more like buyers than sellers," she said. "But either way, we'll keep an eye on them."

Somewhere downstairs a clock chimed. Nancy glanced at her wrist. Eleven o'clock. She was lying in the comfortable brass bed in her hotel room.

She realized that she had had her book open to the same page for almost half an hour. The thought that kept running through her mind was that Ned cared more about Professor Trainey than he did about the truth.

Suddenly she couldn't stand it any longer and put her book down, stood up, and got her jacket from the closet. A little fresh air, maybe a drive, would clear the cobwebs from her mind, she thought.

Nancy headed outside. The night was cold and crisp. As she walked toward the parking lot, she heard voices that sounded familiar.

Just then the headlights of an incoming car swept across a small group of people about fifty feet away. Nancy ducked behind a parked car.

Edith and Gerald Turkower were deep in conversation with Richard and Piker, the two park maintenance men.

Nancy crouched down and began moving between cars to get close enough to hear them. But the group broke up before she got there.

She went back to her room and tried to sort out her thoughts. The only link she could think of between a rich California couple and two Yellowstone maintenance men was poaching. Would any of them know how to track the marmots on the computer? Nancy doubted it. Someone in the camp had to be involved. Someone like Dan Trainey.

Nancy was still thinking when the door opened and Bess rushed in, her face aglow. "The disco was great!" she exclaimed. "And it wasn't even crowded. We had lots of room to dance. You should have come."

Nancy smiled. "Next time."

"Jack is really something!" Bess fell into a chair. "He is totally dedicated to his work and knows absolutely everything about the park. I just hope I can get him as interested in me as he is in whistling marmots," she finished with a laugh.

Nancy smiled. "I get the feeling you had

a good time," she said, then couldn't help sighing.

Bess stared at her. "What's wrong, Nan?"

"It's just that Ned's upset because Dan Trainey is on my list of suspects. I guess he thinks his friends should be exempt from my investigating them."

"That's ridiculous," Bess said. "Ned knows better than that, Nancy. He's just tired and stressed out. He'll feel different tomorrow."

Nancy shook her head. "I hope so," she said.

"Hey, I know," Bess continued. "There's going to be a square dance tomorrow night here at the hotel. Jack asked me to go with him. Why don't you and Ned come, too? We'll have a great time!"

"Good idea," Nancy said, feeling uncomfortable. That was the same dance that Jack had offered to take *her* to just a few hours before. Sure, he had been fooling around, but still . . . Was Jack one of those guys who had to charm every girl he met? If so, Bess was letting herself in for grief. Judging by the gleam in her eye, this was not the time to give her any warnings.

As Nancy and Bess were finishing their breakfast the next morning, Edith Turkower came over to their table. "We're doing a ranger-guided tour of Upper Geyser Basin," she announced. "Gerald and I thought you might like to come along."

Nancy gave Bess a gentle kick on the ankle and said, "I can't, but I know Bess would love to."

As Edith walked away, Nancy said softly, "Keep a close eye on them, Bess. It's important."

"No problem," Bess replied.

Once Bess left the table, Nancy decided to go to the Gardiner hospital to see Brad again. She headed for her car.

Lost in thought, she was already climbing a steep grade on the mountain road that led to Gardiner when she noticed a van close behind her—too close. It seemed to be tailgating her. She pressed harder on the gas pedal, but the van kept pace with her.

The road wound between a sheer wall of rock on the left and a deep ravine on the right. As they came around a long curve, the van pulled out to pass. Nancy edged over toward the ravine to give it more room, but instead of going ahead, the van stayed next to her.

Alarmed, Nancy hit the brakes to let the other vehicle move ahead. Instead, the van slowed.

Then without warning it swerved toward her, its front bumper banging into Nancy's door. She struggled to control the wheel, but the van slammed into her again, forcing her car toward the edge of the ravine.

She glanced to her right, and her stomach twisted. The drop was endless, and she was just about to go over!

Chapter

Six

ALL THAT SEPARATED Nancy from a drop into the ravine was a couple of feet of shoulder, and the van was continuing to nudge her over.

Nancy accelerated, attempting to pull ahead of her pursuer. She knew she couldn't keep driving at this speed—the road was too treacherous.

In seconds the van was behind her again, moving up to slam into her from the rear. She rounded a curve and spotted a sign for a scenic overlook. As she approached it, she took a deep breath and jerked the wheel sharply to the right. The wheels skidded on the gravel.

The van followed and was just about to ram into her again when Nancy saw a tall lodgepole pine at the far end of the overlook parking area. She steered her car straight at it. She was just about to hit it when she swerved left and shot back onto the highway.

In the rearview mirror, she saw the van graze the tree she had just missed. Then, to her astonishment, the driver of the van backed up, turned, and roared off in the other direction.

Puzzled, Nancy stopped her car. When she looked ahead of her, she saw a park service vehicle pulling into the parking area and understood why the driver of the van had headed off in such a hurry. He'd seen the ranger, too.

The ranger stopped his car next to hers and jumped out. He was about forty and had a crewcut and neat mustache. "Are you all right?" he asked.

Nancy nodded, even though she felt shaken. "A van tried to run me off the road."

"Did you see who was driving?" The ranger leaned his elbows on the edge of her window. Nancy noted the name on the plate pinned to his breast pocket: Martin Robbins.

She shook her head.

"Will you come to my office to make a report? It's near the north entrance," he continued.

Nancy followed him back up the road to the ranger station.

Once inside and settled in a chair, she

watched while Robbins filled out a report. "I don't suppose you got the license number?"

Nancy shook her head ruefully. "Sorry, things happened too fast. I did notice the words *Minden Linen* painted on the door of the van. Does that mean anything to you?"

"It's the biggest linen service in this area. All the hotels in Yellowstone get their sheets and towels from there. I know their chief dispatcher. I'll call him," Martin suggested.

Even though she only heard Martin's half of the conversation, Nancy could tell that something was wrong.

"Well?" she asked eagerly once he had hung up.

"One of their drivers, Bert Heckleby, missed a couple of deliveries this morning," Martin replied. "He's not answering calls on his radio either."

Could someone have paid Heckleby to attack her? Or stolen his van?

"I get the feeling that there's more to this than you're telling me," Martin said.

Taking a deep breath, Nancy explained everything, including the propane stove explosion and the missing marmots.

Martin nodded. "Jack's kept me up to date on the problems, but he's not convinced the marmots are being poached. He thinks someone may be trying to sabotage the study."

"That's a possibility," Nancy replied. "But traps and tranquilizers have been stolen. That points to poaching."

The ranger frowned. "I did pass on word of this to the people at the Fish and Wildlife Service," he said. "But there's no telling what they'll do about it. I wish I could help more, but I simply don't have the staff."

After Nancy told Martin that she was a detective, he grinned and nodded appreciatively. "I'd welcome any help you can give, but be careful. Poaching is dangerous business—especially when big money is at stake."

"I understand that whistling marmots can bring as much as five hundred dollars apiece on the black market," Nancy remarked. "If fifty of them really were stolen, the poachers stand to make twenty-five thousand dollars."

Martin glanced above Nancy's shoulder. She turned to see Jack Billings at the open door of the office.

He grinned at her and put a slide projector on the table in the corner of the room. "That ought to work now, Martin. Hey, Nancy. What brings you here?"

"You'd better look after this girl, Jack,"

Martin cautioned. "Somebody doesn't like her. A guy in a van just tried to run her off the road."

"What? Are you serious?" Jack moved closer to Nancy and put his hand on her shoulder solicitously. "Are you okay? You want me to drive you back to the hotel?"

"No need," Nancy replied. "I'm on my way to visit Brad, anyway."

She thanked Martin and then walked outside with Jack. The morning sun glinted against the dent in the side of the white rental car.

"You need to be more careful, Nancy. I'd feel terrible if anything happened to you."

"So would I," she joked. She couldn't help feeling attracted to him, but the warmth and concern she saw in his eyes made her feel awkward. "I'll tell Bess I saw you," she added pointedly.

"Please do. She's a great girl," Jack said, smiling. "I'll see both of you later, right?"

Nancy got into her car and drove off with only a wave for an answer. On the way to the hospital, she kept thinking about Jack. She hoped Bess wasn't getting into something she'd regret.

* * *

Brad's face broke into a welcoming smile when he saw Nancy. "Hi. It's great to see you."

"Hi yourself," she replied, dropping into a chair by the bed. "How are you feeling?"

"Great! The doctor said I'll be out of this place in a day or two."

"I'm glad." Nancy leaned forward. "Listen, Brad, I want to talk about the problems the study's been having. Did you find out anything while you were investigating?"

"The professor is in real financial trouble," Brad replied reluctantly. "I found lots of overdue bills in his tent. You know he's put his own money into this study."

"Yes," Nancy said. "But once the extension comes through, he'll be reimbursed."

"That's just it," Brad said unhappily. "I found a letter from the Department of Interior in his tent. There won't be any extension. Trainey's application was turned down."

"What!" Nancy exclaimed. "That's terrible. That means the professor's out all that money."

Brad nodded. "I'm afraid so."

"Wow!" Nancy thought for a moment. "You know Professor Trainey pretty well, don't you?"

Brad nodded. "I think so. I've worked with him pretty closely for a couple of years."

"Could he be desperate enough to try to get his money back by selling marmots?" Nancy asked.

Brad hesitated for a long time. "I guess he could try to recoup his losses," he said, sighing.

"Does everyone know that you drink a lot of coffee?" Nancy went on.

Brad grinned, glad to change the subject. "Sure. Everybody kids me about always having a cup of the stuff glued to my hand."

"So it would have been a safe assumption that at some point in the evening you would light the stove to boil water?"

"Yes," he confirmed.

"What time did you get to the hut that night?"

"About seven-thirty," Brad replied.

Nancy nodded thoughtfully. The daily assignments were posted outside the command post shed, so everyone would have known that Brad was monitoring feeding station 1. Alicia left the hut around six-thirty. That left the place empty for an hour—plenty of time to sabotage the stove.

"I understand that you and Professor Trainey have the only keys to the command post," Nancy said, turning her thoughts to how the poachers could have gained access to the computer that monitored the marmots' signals.

"Technically, I guess that's true."

Nancy was puzzled. "What do you mean?"

"We had a spare that we kept hidden under a rock near the door—in case we lost the others." Brad laughed. "I guess it wasn't such a great place to hide it, because one morning about two weeks ago we couldn't find it."

Nancy's eyes widened.

Just then a nurse came in to change Brad's bandages. Nancy got up and said, "Well, I guess I'd better go. You've been a great help."

As she drove back to the inn, Nancy's mind was spinning. Who'd taken the key to the command post? Was it someone unconnected to the study group—like the two maintenance men, Piker and Richard?

She felt uneasy every time she thought of them, especially since she'd caught them in the parking lot at the hotel with the Turkowers. Was it possible that the professor, Piker and Richard, and the Turkowers were all involved somehow? It seemed a strange group of people to be working together. Still, she needed to keep her eye on them all.

When Nancy opened the door to her room, she found Bess, bubbling over with enthusiasm. "I had a fabulous morning! Upper Geyser

Basin was amazing. Did you know that Yellowstone sits in the middle of the crater of a gigantic volcano?" She paused and glanced around. "You don't suppose it could erupt again, do you?"

"I doubt it, Bess." Nancy laughed. "What did you find out about the Turkowers?"

Bess wrinkled her forehead. "Gerald must have shot about a hundred pictures, and Edith never stopped talking about her neighbors back in California. But I don't think they're tourists at all. In fact, I'm now betting they're in charge of kidnapping the marmots."

Nancy turned that around in her mind. She had been thinking of the Turkowers as buyers who might lead her to the poaching ring. What if Bess was right, though, and they were the sellers instead?

"But wait," Bess added. "I haven't told you my most exciting news. Guess who's coming to Yellowstone Park?"

"Smokey the Bear?" Nancy suggested.

Bess threw a pillow at her.

"Okay," she said. "I give up."

"You'll never believe it," Bess cried, her eyes wide with excitement. "Randy Dean!"

Chapter

Seven

REALLY? Randy Dean here?" Nancy said. "Are you sure?"

Bess nodded emphatically. "Uh-huh. The ranger told us this morning. He's coming to make a television special about the importance of leaving animals in their natural environments."

"Oh? What about all those marmots of his?" Nancy asked.

Bess shrugged. "He must have had a change of heart." Her face lit up again. "And not only that, he's going to be staying right in this hotel. We might even meet him! Wouldn't that be awesome? George is going to be so jealous when she hears."

"We haven't met him yet," Nancy pointed

out. To herself, she wondered about the rock star's change of heart. Was it for real or simply a good excuse for a TV special? "I had a rather eventful morning myself, Bess."

She told her friend about what Brad had said and the attempt to run her off the road.

"Nan, that's terrible!" Bess exclaimed. "You could have been killed!"

"Well, I wasn't. And the main thing is, this attack shows that we're on the right track. The poachers are getting desperate."

"So what's our next move?" Bess asked.

"Lunch," Nancy said firmly. "I don't know about you, but I'm starved."

Downstairs, they found the dining room crowded. As they were waiting by the hostess station, Edith and Gerald Turkower came in.

"Well, hello again," Edith said with a smile.

Just then the hostess came over. "I have a table for four by the window," she announced.

"Wonderful," Edith said brightly. "Why don't we all eat together?"

"Sure," Nancy replied. Here was a perfect opportunity to find out more about the Turkowers.

The hostess led them to a round oak table near the window and handed them menus.

"The cutthroat trout caught in the Yellowstone Lake are supposed to be the best in the world," Gerald told them, placing his cameras on the windowsill.

"Really?" Bess closed her menu. "I'll try it."

"So will I," Nancy said.

"I'll just have the vegetarian platter," Edith said. "It's a little chilly in here, don't you think?" she added, slipping into a beige sweater with a fur collar.

The waitress came and took their orders. As she left, Nancy asked casually, "How's the hunt for whistling marmots going?"

Edith made a face. "Not very well. We haven't even seen one yet."

"What about you, any luck?" Gerald asked.

"Why, yes," Nancy replied. "There's a research group here studying the marmots. I visited their camp yesterday and saw a couple of them at one of the feeding stations. They're every bit as cute as I expected, too."

Nancy paused as the waitress placed bowls of green salad in front of everyone.

Nancy picked up her fork and took a bite of salad. Then, leaning forward, she lowered her voice. "A guy from the group told me that some of the marmots are missing."

She scrutinized the Turkowers and thought she saw an uneasy expression in Gerald's eyes.

"Do you think someone is stealing them?" he asked.

Nancy shrugged. "I have no idea."

Gerald put down his fork. "I suppose it's possible that someone on the Emerson team might be stealing marmots," he mused. "College students are always short of cash."

Nancy's breath caught in her throat. She had never mentioned Emerson College!

Had Gerald noticed her reaction? With a wary expression, he added, "I think I saw an article about that research project. Maybe we should pay them a visit. Edith won't be happy until she's had a chance to watch the little critters in action." He beamed fondly at his wife and winked.

Edith smiled back at him. "In some ways," she began, "a marmot would be better off with us than in the wild. We'd give it such a good home," she cooed. "Gerald and I are staunch animal rights supporters. Why, I've even become a vegetarian."

Nancy noticed the startled expression on Bess's face, but before she could figure out what caused it, their broiled trout had arrived.

After lunch the Turkowers excused themselves, saying they planned to drive to Yellowstone Lake.

"That couple is definitely phony," Bess said in the main lobby.

"What makes you say that?" Nancy asked.

Bess rolled her eyes. "If Edith is so into animal rights," she demanded, "why was she wearing a sweater with a mink collar?"

"Maybe it was fake fur," Nancy suggested.

"No way!" Bess scoffed. "I can tell the difference, believe me."

"Come on, Bess. I just saw the Turkowers head out the front door. I want to check out their room."

Nancy led the way to the house phones and asked the switchboard for the Turkowers. After half a dozen rings, the operator said, "Sorry, Room three twenty-six doesn't answer."

Nancy and Bess climbed the stairs to the third floor. At the Turkowers' door, Nancy rapped lightly, then tried the knob. It was locked. After a quick glance up and down the hall, she pulled a small case of lockpicks from her shoulder bag and went to work. A few moments later the door sprang open.

"Bess, you stand guard while I search the room," Nancy said. Bess nodded and Nancy slipped inside.

Like the room Nancy and Bess were sharing, this one had rough-hewn plank walls, brass beds, and an old-fashioned washstand complete with porcelain bowl and pitcher. The window looked out onto a steaming geyser field.

Nancy opened the oak wardrobe in the corner. The right side held women's clothes. To her amazement, there were only three outfits hanging there. Nancy had expected Edith to be like Bess and bring virtually everything she owned.

She moved to the dresser and started pulling drawers open. Quickly, she riffled through a pile of men's shirts and sweaters. She came up empty-handed.

As she pushed the drawer closed, she noticed that it seemed to be sticking. She pulled it all the way out and held it up so she could see the underside. There was a manila envelope taped to the bottom of the drawer.

Carefully removing it, she opened the envelope and pulled out a sheet of fax paper. There were no headings, simply a list of animals, each followed by a dollar amount and one or two locations. She scanned the list, her eyes stopping at an entry that said: "Whistling Marmot—$400–$500—Yellowstone Park." Someone had inked a little star next to it.

Shocked, Nancy realized that she was looking at a list of how much wild animals would bring on the black market.

Taking care not to crease the fragile sheet, Nancy put it back in the envelope and retaped it to the underside of the drawer. Then she took one last peek at the room to make sure she hadn't left anything out of place and slipped out the door.

On the way downstairs, she told Bess what she had found.

"Well, that settles it," Bess declared. "I knew right from the start that Edith and Gerald weren't ordinary tourists. They're in the marmot black market up to their necks."

Nancy frowned. "I still think someone from the Emerson group has to be involved, too. All the thefts, not to mention Brad's and Ned's injuries, point to an inside job."

"What's next, Nan?" Bess asked.

"Let's head out and find Richard and Piker. I want to ask them a few questions about what they were discussing with the Turkowers," she said.

Bess rolled down her car window, but the breeze was too chilly, so she put it up again.

The road led along the bank of the Firehole River, kept warm by the hot springs in its bed. A layer of white mist hid the surface of the water. Nancy slowed down as they passed the Fountain Paint Pots, a series of pools turned vivid colors by the algae that lived in them. All at once she hit the brakes.

"What is it?" Bess asked, alarmed. "Is something wrong?"

"Look—in the middle of those aspens," Nancy replied, pointing.

"What is it?" Bess repeated. "A bear?"

"No, it's a van," Nancy said. "And if I'm not mistaken, it's the same one that tried to run me off the road this morning."

"Are you sure?" Bess gasped.

Nancy nodded and pulled onto the shoulder of the road. Getting out, she walked down a dirt trail toward the half-concealed van. As she approached, she saw the words *Minden Linen* painted on the side.

"This is it," she said over her shoulder. "You can see the dent where it grazed off the tree. And look." She pointed to a streak of white paint on the bumper. "That's from our car."

Bess glanced around nervously. "Do you think the people who did it are still around?"

"I doubt it," Nancy said. She pulled open the driver's side door and peered inside. The keys were in the ignition. "I'm going to search the cab. Keep an eye out for me, okay?"

"Just make it quick," Bess urged.

Hastily Nancy climbed into the cab and opened the glove compartment. She found nothing except the registration and insurance card, both issued to the linen supply company. Under the seat, she found a creased map of the park. She was climbing out when she suddenly heard a thumping sound.

Beth paled. "Nancy, let's get out of here."

The sound came again, louder this time.

"There's someone in the back of the van!" Nancy exclaimed. She ran around to the rear doors and yanked the handle down. It was locked. "Bess, grab the keys. They're in the ignition."

Bess grabbed the large key ring, then dashed back to Nancy with it. The third key worked, and she yanked the door open.

The van was piled with neatly folded linen, and lying on a pile of towels in the center was a middle-aged man with round, wild eyes. His hands and feet were tied, and in his mouth was a gag.

Chapter

Eight

N<small>ANCY AND</small> B<small>ESS</small> scrambled into the van and quickly released the man.

"Mr. Heckleby?" Nancy inquired as the man rubbed his chafed wrists. He nodded.

"Are you all right?" Bess asked.

"I've been better," he replied, massaging his ankles. "But I sure am glad you came along. I've been tied up for hours."

"What happened?" Nancy asked.

Heckleby pushed back his unruly gray hair. "Beats me," he said. "I was driving along near Madison Junction when I saw a car blocking the road. I stopped and got out to see if I could help, and someone grabbed me from behind. I felt something jab my arm. When I woke up I was hogtied and gagged on the floor of the van."

"You must have been drugged!" Nancy exclaimed. "Whoever it was hijacked your truck and tried to run me off the road with it."

"Who would do a thing like that? And why?" he demanded.

"I don't know," Nancy replied, remembering the missing syringes and tranquilizer vials at the campsite.

The girls helped Heckleby out of the van. "I'd better call the office and have them get a ranger over here." He reached into the cab for his radio.

Less than ten minutes later a park service cruiser pulled up behind Nancy's car and two officers got out. They introduced themselves as Rangers Dillon and Cramer and took statements from both Nancy and Heckleby.

Before leaving, the officers offered to drive Heckleby to the hospital in Gardiner, but he said he was too far behind on his rounds already. After thanking Nancy and Bess for rescuing him, he got into the van and drove off.

Nancy was silent as she started the car and swung onto the road.

"What are you thinking, Nan?" Bess asked.

Nancy told her about the syringes.

"You think someone from Ned's group drugged Mr. Heckleby and tried to kill you?"

"I can't really narrow it down that far," Nancy replied slowly. "Anyone could have taken the spare key to the command post."

Nancy drove past Madison Junction toward the Emerson campsite. "We need to find out where everyone was this morning around ten. That's when I was forced off the road."

"I'll do my best," Bess promised.

As Nancy got out of the car, she heard hammering. Squinting against the afternoon sun, she spotted Richard and Piker about fifty yards away. "Come on," she said to Bess in a low voice. They approached the workers, who were lining up long, smooth planks of wood and nailing them to stout crosspieces.

"Hi!" Bess called gaily. "Building a new walkway?"

The two men raised their heads. Piker's face was expressionless, but Richard gave Bess a slight grin. "Yeah," he answered.

"Why here?" Bess asked. "There aren't any geysers around, are there?"

"Princess Geyser is about a half mile north," Richard explained.

"This looks like a big job," Nancy commented. "How long have you been at it?"

"Since first thing this morning," he said. "Why?"

Nancy acted puzzled. "No reason, except that I thought I saw you in Gardiner this morning."

Richard chuckled. "Must have been my double, because I've been here all day."

Nancy and Bess headed through the woods to the campsite. Jack was beside the command post, checking out the assignment sheet. When he saw them, he smiled and yelled, "Well, hello there."

His gaze moved warmly from Nancy to Bess and back again. Bess moved close to him and said, "Hello yourself. It seems like ages since I saw you. Have you been having an exciting day?"

Nancy smothered a laugh. Bess might be falling in love, but as promised, she was trying to help out with the case.

"Oh, very exciting," Jack replied, his smile broadening. "This morning Ned and I started packing up station four. Then came the high point—I repaired a park service slide projector. I tell you, the life of a park ranger is full of thrills!"

Bess giggled.

"Is Ned still around?" Nancy asked.

"He was up at feeding station one a while back," Jack told her.

"I think I'll hike up there," Nancy told Bess.

"Go ahead," she replied. "I'll stay here."

Nancy was about halfway up the hill when she heard a shrill whistling sound. Startled, she stopped and looked around. It came again from a clump of bushes about sixty feet to the left of the path. She made her way there and cautiously parted the scraggly branches, then let out a cry.

Under the bushes was a wire trap just like the one Ned had showed her the day before. Inside was a little marmot. One of its hind legs was caught in the door and was badly swollen.

Nancy's first impulse was to run for help, but she couldn't bear to leave the suffering creature. She knew that handling an injured animal could be dangerous, so she took the scarf from around her neck and wrapped it around her hand. Even if the marmot tried to bite her, the scarf would keep its teeth from breaking her skin. She knelt down and opened the door, gingerly freeing the marmot's leg.

"There, there," she crooned as she slowly withdrew her hand. "You'll be all right now."

Just then she heard Bess's voice shouting. "Nancy, where are you?"

"Over here," Nancy yelled. She shut the

cage door and stood up as Bess and Jack came hurrying up the path.

Bess was huffing when she reached Nancy's side. "What happened? We heard a terrible noise."

Jack came to a stop behind Bess. "I told her it was a marmot," he said.

"You're right, it is a marmot. See? Its leg was caught in the trap."

"Oh, no!" Bess gasped. "Is it badly hurt?"

Jack bent down and carefully examined the animal, then stood up, his face angry. "His leg's not broken, but he's definitely hurt," he told them. "Let's take him back to camp. We'll clean the cut and bandage it."

"Can I help, Jack?" Bess asked, her eyes fixed on the injured animal.

"Of course." Jack's face relaxed into a smile. "With a pretty angel of mercy like you, this little guy will recover in no time."

"Are you coming, Nancy?" Bess asked.

Nancy shook her head. "I'm going up to the feeding station to see if Ned's still there." As she made her way up the hill, she kept thinking about the marmot. Had the thieves overlooked that trap when they collected the other marmots, or were they starting to trap more?

When she approached the fenced-off area, she saw Ned and Jennifer, their heads close together, making some adjustments to one of the time-lapse cameras. The sight made her a little uneasy. She took a deep breath, pasted a confident smile on her face, and called out, "Hi, guys."

"Nancy!" Ned dashed over and gave her a big hug and a quick kiss.

Nancy's spirits soared; Ned wasn't angry with her any longer. She turned to find Jennifer watching them, a hint of challenge in her eyes.

"I can finish up here by myself if you want to take a break," Jennifer said. "We got a lot accomplished today. Nancy, will you be at the square dance tonight? It should be lots of fun. Ned, don't forget you promised me a Virginia reel."

Ned shifted his feet uncomfortably. "Oh, I won't," he said, then turned to Nancy. "I worked straight through lunch, so I'm due an hour or so. You want to drive to Mammoth Hot Springs? It's my favorite place in the park."

She touched his arm lightly. "That would be great." They walked down the hill and stopped at the campsite to tell Bess and Jack where she was going. Bess was so occupied with helping Jack that she only nodded.

Ned led Nancy to one of the camp's Jeeps.

The top was down so Nancy zipped up her jacket before climbing in.

During the twenty-minute drive, Nancy told Ned everything that had happened since she'd last seen him. She mentioned the Turkowers, the attack on the road, and how she'd found the linen service driver bound and gagged in his van.

Ned was appalled to learn how close Nancy had come to being run off the road. "You've got to be more careful, Nan," he said anxiously. "I don't know what I'd do if anything happened to you."

She felt a sudden glow. "Don't worry. I know what I'm doing," she told him. "And anyway, what about you? I'm not the one who got himself knocked out. How's your head today?"

Ned lifted one hand from the wheel to touch the back of his head, where it was bandaged. "It's still there," he joked. "I can take this bandage off tomorrow, though."

"I hope you've been taking it easy."

"Are you kidding?" he exclaimed. "We have to wrap up everything by Saturday. I've been going like crazy since daybreak. We all have."

He pulled the Jeep onto an embankment and parked. "Come on," he said, pocketing the keys. "From here we walk."

They crossed the road and made their way up the path.

"Mammoth Hot Springs is a twenty-foot-high stack of limestone with one side cut away by erosion," Ned told her. "And it's gorgeous. Look."

Nancy gasped in delight as they cleared the trees, and she saw steaming water flowing softly down a series of stone terraces that looked like giant multicolored steps. Near the top the stones were pure white, but farther down they were splashed with red, brown, pink, and tan.

"At the top the water is so hot that nothing can live on the stones," Ned told her. "But the water cools off as it flows downward, allowing algae to grow on the lower terraces. That's why those ledges are so many different colors."

"It's beautiful!" Nancy exclaimed.

"I wanted to be sure you saw this," he said, putting his arm around her waist. "But I'm afraid I have to get right back to camp. You can't imagine how much work we still have to do."

After another long look at the limestone terraces, they reluctantly headed back to the car.

"How's the case going, Nancy?" Ned asked as he drove back to the campsite.

"I'm making some progress, but not a lot," she said. "I've got too many suspects. Anyone could have taken the key from under the rock by the command post, which means I have to consider outsiders, like Piker and Richard."

Ned nodded. "Well, if the key was stolen, Professor Trainey obviously didn't do it. He's got one of his own."

Nancy remained silent for a moment, then told Ned the news about the grant extension. He looked crushed. "Dan didn't say a word about it," he began. "I guess he's too upset."

"It's awful, I know," Nancy said carefully. "And I'm afraid I've still got to watch the professor. He must be pretty desperate for money now."

Ned's knuckles whitened as he gripped the wheel tighter. "That's ridiculous. Professor Trainey is the last person on earth who'd get involved in poaching marmots—no matter how hard up he is," he said indignantly.

Nancy took a deep breath. "Try to see it objectively. He's got a strong motive. And he has complete access to the equipment. I can't rule him out on your say-so."

Ned was silent for a long time. As he pulled into the parking area, he finally spoke. "I'm beginning to wish I'd never asked you to help. Some help! Doesn't the poor guy have enough problems just trying to get this part of the project completed by Saturday? If you can't manage to leave Dan Trainey alone, you'd better just turn around and go back to River Heights!"

Nancy's anger spoke for her. "I don't think you want this case solved! You're more interested in protecting your precious professor and not offending dear Jennifer than you are in finding out who's been poaching marmots."

"At least Jennifer pays attention to what I say," Ned retorted hotly.

Nancy knew, even as the words rose to her lips, that she was going to regret them. She couldn't stop herself though. "Is Jennifer willing to shut her eyes to the truth just because you tell her to?" she demanded. "Then all I can say, Ned Nickerson, is that the two of you deserve each other!"

Chapter

Nine

If THAT'S THE WAY you feel, I guess I know what to do about it!" Ned jumped out of the Jeep and stomped away.

Nancy sat still. What had Ned meant? Did he want to break up?

She started to follow him up to the campsite but then checked her steps. Maybe she should wait a bit to give him a chance to cool off. In the meantime she decided to talk to Bess.

Nancy found her at feeding station 1, stroking the injured marmot through the bars of its cage.

"Oh, Nancy," Bess said, "look at Spike. Isn't he adorable?" Her blue eyes sparkled with enthusiasm.

In spite of the way she felt, Nancy managed a faint smile. "Spike?"

"I call him that because of the way his fur stands up around his head," Bess explained. "Look, Jack bandaged Spike's leg while I held him. The little guy didn't even try to bite me. So how did things go with Ned?" Bess asked, glancing at her. Then she quickly added, "Uh-oh. Not so well, huh?"

"No," Nancy said. She gave Bess a full account of their most recent argument, including their parting words.

"That doesn't sound good," Bess replied, frowning. "But you don't really think that Ned and Jennifer . . ."

"I don't know what to think," Nancy said. "They've been together every day for two and a half weeks now. But I'm sorry I said what I did—even if I meant every word of it!"

Nancy heard footsteps. Hoping it was Ned, she spun around eagerly. It was Professor Trainey. She couldn't help letting out a sigh of disappointment.

Trainey nodded to her and gave Bess a distracted glance, then bent down to peer inside the cage. "This must be the little fellow Jack told me about," he said.

"He's so cute," Bess announced. "Maybe in my next life I'll come back as a marmot."

Trainey actually smiled at her—it was the first time Nancy had seen him happy.

Bess turned to Nancy and said, "Come on, let's go check out a few sights while the light's still good. We'll have plenty of time to eat dinner and change before the square dance."

Nancy sighed and said, "I'll probably skip the dance."

Bess gave her a sharp glance, then replied, "We can discuss that later. Right now, what do you say to a waterfall?" Without waiting for an answer, Bess hooked her arm in Nancy's to lead her down to the car.

After a few minutes of driving, Nancy said, "Bess? I think somebody's following us. A dark blue car's been right behind us the whole time." All at once the car pulled off at a scenic overlook. "So much for that," Nancy said with a laugh. "I guess I'm getting paranoid."

Bess reached over to touch her shoulder. "Nancy?" she said in a tentative voice. "Are you positive that the professor is involved in the poaching?"

"Positive? Of course not," Nancy replied, surprised by the question. "I don't have evidence to prove it either way. Brad says he saw him just before his accident—but he wasn't positive. And then there was that Phi Beta Kappa key."

"Then he *is* your chief suspect."

"Well," Nancy said slowly, "no one is in a better position to set up a poaching operation than he is. . . ."

"What happens if we don't find the missing marmots?" Bess asked. "Or if more of them disappear?"

"I guess the study will be ruined—and so will the professor's career," Nancy answered.

"So poaching and selling marmots wouldn't exactly solve his problem," Bess went on. "In some ways, it would only make it worse."

Nancy nodded. "I see what you mean, Bess." Nancy's thoughts were churning. *Was* she focusing too hard on Trainey? In that case she owed Ned an apology—if she could ever get him to listen to it.

She slowed the car down. "There's a sign for the falls," she announced.

After finding a spot in the crowded parking area, Nancy and Bess followed a sawdust-covered path through the woods. As they walked, they heard a low, persistent rumble in the distance. When they emerged from the trees at the base of the falls, the sound was overwhelming.

Bess tapped Nancy's arm. Nancy turned and saw her friend's lips moving but couldn't hear anything above the roar of the water. Bess pointed up the path and raised an eyebrow. Nancy nodded and followed her friend to an observation platform perched a dozen feet above the river, just beyond the reach of the spray.

She craned her neck to peer up at the top, where the water cascaded over a ridge of red and yellow volcanic rock. The constant motion of the water made her feel a little dizzy, so she clutched the railing for support.

Bess leaned her head close to Nancy's. "Would you like the binoculars?" she shouted, holding them out. Nancy took them and could see the individual droplets of water splashing into the river. Along the banks, bright wildflowers grew.

A large group of sightseers jostled onto the platform behind Nancy. Two middle-aged women pushed up and flanked her. As her gaze swept farther down the riverbank, she noticed a man with black hair. Frowning, she focused the binoculars to get a clearer image. She let out a gasp because she was looking at Dan Trainey, who was holding a marmot trap!

Nancy focused in tighter and realized that Trainey was talking to someone who was partly hidden by a tree trunk. All she could make out were the other person's hands gesturing to Trainey.

She wanted to get a better view, so she started edging her way along the railing. She had almost reached the corner of the platform when someone shouted, "Look! A red-tailed hawk!"

As the crowd on the platform surged forward, Nancy felt someone put both hands on her back and give her a powerful shove. A moment later she was falling over the rail into the swirling river below.

Chapter

Ten

NANCY GASPED as she hit the icy water. She had just enough time to fill her lungs and clamp her mouth shut before the river swirled over her. She fought her way to the surface and tried to make it to the nearest bank, but the raging current pulled her downstream.

As an eddy spun her around, she got one last glimpse of the platform she had just been pushed from and saw Bess frantically making her way through the stunned crowd, trying to reach the riverbank.

The current tumbled her again, pushing her into a somersault. Nancy flailed her arms wildly and managed to keep her head up, but she didn't know how much longer she could hold on.

Downstream, a boulder rose up above the surface about half a dozen feet from shore. If only she could get to it, she thought, she might have a chance of saving herself.

Nancy put all the energy and determination she had into powerful strokes and kicks. Just as she was sure she couldn't keep it up any longer, the rock was right in front of her. She wrapped her arms around it and took a deep breath.

"Nancy! Over here!"

Startled, she looked over and saw Gerald Turkower standing on the riverbank near her.

"Hang on!" he shouted, cautiously stepping off the bank. He inched forward, the water swirling around his knees now, then leaned forward and stretched out his hand. Nancy reached out and grasped it. Gerald steadied himself, then reeled Nancy in to the bank as if she were one of those cutthroat trout he had talked about at lunch.

Nancy's legs were numb and wouldn't hold her up. "Thanks," she said to Gerald through chattering teeth.

"Nancy! Are you all right?" Bess demanded, running up.

"C-c-cold" was all Nancy could manage.

Gerald took off his fleece-lined leather jacket and draped it around Nancy's shoulders.

Bess turned to him. "Where did you come from?" she asked curiously.

His eyes flickered. "I was in the woods, taking pictures."

Nancy looked sharply at him and struggled to find her voice. "Was anybody with you?" she asked after a second.

Gerald shook his head. "Come on, Nancy, I'll help you to your car. You need to get in and turn the heater on full blast. How did you happen to fall in?" he asked as they walked.

"I didn't," she replied. "Somebody pushed me."

"What?" Gerald's face registered shock. "Are you sure? Couldn't you just have been jostled?"

Nancy shook her head. "I distinctly felt two hands shoving against my back. It was no accident, take my word for it. Did you see anything, Bess?"

"No. I'm sorry," Bess replied on the verge of tears. "I was looking at the falls."

"Don't worry about it," Nancy said. "You had no reason to think somebody was going to push me in."

As they reached the car, Gerald told Nancy to go back to the hotel and take a hot shower.

"I'll drive, Nan," Bess offered. "You relax."

Nancy gave Bess the keys, then thanked Gerald again for rescuing her.

"I'm glad I was there to help," he replied, holding the door for her.

Bess turned on the heater, and soon Nancy stopped shivering. "It was a man who pushed me," she said. "As I went over the railing, I got an impression of his hands. They were too big and hairy to belong to a woman. Oh, Bess," Nancy said, interrupting herself. "Your binoculars! They must have fallen into the river with me. I'm so sorry."

"Do you think I care about some old binoculars when I just watched you nearly drown?" Bess scolded.

As Bess turned into the hotel parking lot, she continued, "Who could have pushed you?"

"I don't know. I just don't know. In fact, I don't know what to think anymore."

A large, shiny bus was stopped in front of the hotel entrance. People were spilling out of it onto the sidewalk.

"Look, Nancy," Bess said excitedly, pointing out the bus, which said Randy Dean Productions. "Do you think Randy's with them?" she asked.

Nancy smiled. "I doubt if a big star like Randy Dean would arrive on a bus," she said. "He's probably coming by private helicopter."

"I guess you're right," Bess said, parking the car. "Come on, let's get you inside and warm."

Nancy's legs felt like lead as she climbed the steps to the hotel lobby. "All I want to do is lie down in a warm tub and soak for a month or two," she announced as Bess unlocked the door to their room.

Bess gave her a concerned look. "Are you sure you don't want to see a doctor?"

"I'm sure," Nancy replied firmly. "After a hot bath and a little rest, I'll be as good as new."

At Bess's urging, the girls had dinner in their room. As the waiter took away the tray, Bess gave Nancy a close look and said, "You look a lot better. You may not be up for an evening of square dancing, but at least you can sit and watch."

"You really think I ought to go?" Nancy asked.

Bess was now standing in front of the mirror, smoothing the waist of her knee-length denim skirt. "You want to see Ned, don't you?"

"Of course I do," Nancy replied, then paused. "But I don't know what to say to him."

Bess spun around, went to Nancy, and sat

beside her on the bed. "First you'll tell him you're sorry," she stated flatly. "Then you'll say that you love him. Then he'll take you for a moonlight drive . . ." Bess giggled. "And I'm not going to say what happens after that."

Nancy shook her head sadly. "I only wish it could be that easy."

Bess gave Nancy a hug. "Stop worrying. It's going to be fine."

While Nancy pulled on a full-skirted blue corduroy dress, Bess went on. "I talked to Jack while you were napping. He'll meet us in the lobby at eight."

"'Us'?" Nancy repeated.

"Well, sure," Bess said. "This is a group event, you know, not a date."

When they reached the head of the stairs, Bess began searching through her purse. "I forgot my compact," she said. "I've got to go back."

"Okay," Nancy said. "I'll meet you in the lobby."

Jack, in worn but perfectly fitting jeans and a red plaid shirt, was standing near the foot of the stairs. He saw Nancy coming and gave her a warm smile. "I called Bess after you got back to the hotel, and she told me what happened," he said, concerned. "Are you all right?"

"Good as new," Nancy said. "Bess will be down in a minute."

She took in the transformed lobby. All the furniture had been cleared away from the central area, and a small stage had been set up near the windows. Paper lanterns dangled from the log rafters, and bales of hay had been placed along the walls.

"They did a great job of decorating this place, didn't they?" Jack said, and led the way to a table at the edge of the dance floor. "I'm glad you felt well enough to come. I've been really looking forward to the dance," he added with a glance full of meaning.

"So has Bess," Nancy replied pointedly as she spotted her friend coming down the stairs.

Jack sprang to his feet as Bess approached. "Hey, you look terrific!"

Bess blushed becomingly and threw in a little curtsy.

The other tables were filling up. Two men and a woman in matching shirts climbed up on the stage and started tuning a guitar, fiddle, and string bass.

A woman in a fringed leather vest joined the trio on stage and picked up a microphone. "Okay, folks," she said. "We're going to start out real easy this evening. You don't need a

95

partner for this one. Don't be shy, just form two long lines, gents on the left and ladies on the right. The name of the tune is 'Rabbit in the Peapatch.'"

"Come on, you two," Jack urged, springing up. As the band launched into the rollicking tune, Nancy saw Ned and Jennifer come in the door. Jennifer was pulling Ned toward the two lines of dancers.

As he passed, Ned spotted Nancy and smiled at her tentatively. Then the dance started, and Nancy was too busy following the caller's instructions to pay attention to Ned.

"This is fun!" Bess exclaimed breathlessly when the first number ended.

Nancy smiled, but her eyes were now searching for Ned. There he was, she thought, near the stage. He was looking around, too. For her? Taking a deep breath, Nancy crossed the room.

"Hi, Ned," she said.

He didn't say a word, only took her hand and led her off to the far side of the fireplace.

They turned to face each other. Nancy could hear the music start for the next dance, but the only thing that mattered now was Ned.

He was staring down at the floor. She was

about to say something when he spoke up. "I really lost it this afternoon," he said, his brown eyes shining. "I'm sorry, Nan. You know I didn't mean those things I said."

"Of course I do," Nancy responded. "I said things I didn't mean, too, and I'm sorry. I really do understand the way you feel about Professor Trainey. It's just that—"

"It's just that you're too good a detective not to follow up on all the evidence you find, no matter where it leads," he finished. "And I wouldn't want you any different."

Nancy put her arms around his neck. "Oh, Ned—I'm so glad you understand." She pulled his head down to hers, and their lips met in a kiss that lasted a long time.

When they parted, Ned held her close and ran his fingers through her hair. "Why don't we get our coats and go for a drive?" he said breathlessly. "It's a beautiful night."

"I'd love it," Nancy replied.

They were walking past the alcove that held the house phones when Ned squeezed her elbow. He put his finger to his lips and pulled her back out of sight.

"Gerry? It's me." Nancy recognized Professor Trainey's voice. She strained to make out the words.

"Yes, I know," she heard the professor say into the phone. "It can't be helped. Late tomorrow night? Yes, the camp should be quiet. No junior detectives to get in our way."

Chapter

Eleven

NANCY HEARD Trainey hang up and then watched him walk away.

Ned was slumped against the wall, his eyes filled with misery. He stared at her. "You were right about the professor all along."

The bitterness in his voice surprised Nancy. Her heart ached for him. "I'm sorry, Ned," she said, slipping her arms around him. "I kept hoping it wasn't him, but—"

"'Junior detectives,'" Ned spat out. "And I kept telling you how much he respected and cared about his students. He thinks we're a joke!"

"He must be pretty desperate," Nancy pointed out. "I don't think he would have gotten involved if it weren't for his money problems. And let's face it—if he *is* involved, our investigation must really be getting in his way."

Ned's eyes widened. *"If?* Of course he's involved. You heard what he said. He's planning something for tomorrow night. And he was talking to Turkower!"

Nancy remained impassive. "I've got to admit, that surprises me," she began slowly. "After what Gerald did today to save me, I was starting to think he was okay."

Ned was obviously confused, and Nancy realized that she hadn't told him about her dip into the river. She took a deep breath and told the whole story. "Gerald pulled me out," she concluded.

"I just can't believe that someone I admired so much could be involved in something so awful." Ned shook his head. "Trainey is such a hypocrite."

Nancy stepped back. "Look, Ned. I don't have any real proof against the professor, just what Brad said, so let's not jump to conclusions. What I really need to do is catch the poachers in the act, and it sounds like I might be able to do that tomorrow night."

Ned brightened a little. "Are you still up for

that drive?" he asked. "I know I am. I'm sick of thinking about this mess."

"I'll run upstairs for my jacket," Nancy replied.

When she came back down dressed for the outdoors she waved goodbye to Bess, who was dancing in a square with Jack. Her friend gave her a big grin, then Nancy went out to the parking lot. It was quite chilly, and she was glad to see that Ned had put the top up.

"Feel like looking at the moon from the shore of Yellowstone Lake," he asked her softly as he started the Jeep.

On an impulse Nancy leaned over and kissed him on the cheek.

He reached over and squeezed her hand. "Will you forgive me for being so pigheaded?"

"I already have, Ned."

They'd just turned onto the parkway that ran beside the lake when Nancy said, "Ned, look. Somebody's in trouble."

Parked on the opposite shoulder was a low-slung Italian sports car. The driver was standing with a flashlight pointed under the raised hood.

Ned pulled over and then carefully turned around so he could light up the sports car. He leaned out and called, "Need help?"

The driver moving toward them was very familiar. They had both seen that face on countless posters and CDs.

"Is that who I think it is?" Ned said to Nancy.

Nancy studied the man's liquid brown eyes and curly, honey-colored hair. "It is. It's Randy Dean!"

"Hi there!" Randy stopped next to Ned's door and leaned over to peer into the window. "Thanks for coming to my rescue."

"You have car trouble?" Ned asked.

The rock star shrugged. "It looks that way. I went over a big bump a while back and heard a loud thump. Then, about half a mile back, the engine started sputtering. Now it's stopped. Do you know anything about cars?"

"We both know a little," Ned replied. "We can take a look if you'd like."

"Great." Randy backed away, and Ned and Nancy got out of the Jeep. He held his hand out to Ned. "I'm Randy Dean."

Ned grinned. "Yeah, we figured that out. I'm Ned Nickerson and this is Nancy Drew."

"Hi, Nancy." She was surprised at how personable and open Randy seemed.

Ned reached for Randy's flashlight, clicked it on, and peered under the hood. Nancy joined him.

They poked around under the hood for a few minutes, then Ned said, "I don't know what's wrong. Let me see if I can start it."

Ned climbed into the driver's seat, but when he turned the key in the ignition, the engine only coughed and sputtered.

Nancy leaned inside and looked at the array of gauges on the dashboard. "Did you know you're out of gas?"

Randy frowned. "That's impossible. I filled the tank just an hour ago."

Ned got down on the ground and shone the flashlight under the car. "You've got a leak in your fuel line," he reported. "It must have happened when you hit that bump. All your gas has leaked out," he said, getting up and slapping his palms against his jeans.

Ned offered to take Randy to the hotel. The rock star transferred his luggage from the tiny trunk of the sports car to the Jeep and climbed into the backseat next to it.

"I read a magazine article about you the other night," Nancy said casually. "It mentioned that you collect whistling marmots."

"I used to have quite a few of them," Randy admitted. "They make fun pets. But I don't collect them anymore."

"Why not?" Nancy asked.

"I realized how wrong it is to take animals

out of the wild," he replied earnestly. "In fact, that's why I'm here. I'm doing a TV program on the importance of protecting wild animals and their habitats. Would you guys like to come watch us film?"

"We'd love to," Nancy promptly replied. "Do you think I could bring a friend, too? She's a big fan of yours."

Ned pulled into the hotel parking lot.

"Of course you can," Randy said. "I'll write a note to the production crew as soon as I get upstairs. Thanks for everything. I would have had to sit out there all night."

"Glad we could help," Ned replied. He gave Randy a hand carrying his luggage into the lobby while Nancy parked the Jeep.

The square dance was still going on as Nancy and Ned found a quiet spot and settled down on a couch on the far side of the big room.

"I keep thinking about that phone call," Ned said. "You think the Turkowers are the buyers?"

"It seems that way."

"What do you think they're arranging for tomorrow night?" he asked.

"My hunch is that Trainey's going to turn over the marmots he's already captured to the Turkowers."

Ned acted surprised. "You think the animals are still in the park?"

"Yes, I do," Nancy said. "If they weren't, why would the Turkowers be hanging around? And I'll bet they're being kept somewhere fairly close to the campsite, too."

"So what's our next move?"

"We have to keep our eyes on the Turkowers and Trainey—and I'm still interested in Piker and Richard. It could be that the professor hired them to do the rough work," she speculated. "But the main thing is, it's obvious that this whole case is centered at your camp. We can't hope to solve it if I'm always somewhere else. I think it's time Bess and I move to the campsite."

"So you and Bess are going to camp." Ned grinned. "I'd love to be there when you break the news to her."

Nancy grimaced. "Do you have any idea what we can do about equipment? We'll need a tent and sleeping bags at least."

"There are outfitters in West Yellowstone and Jackson that sell camping gear. But why not ask Martin Robbins at the ranger station? I bet he could lend you what you need."

"Good idea," she said.

He put his arm around Nancy's shoulders, and she settled back against him. "I'm glad you're moving to the camp," he continued softly. "Having you so near will be the only bright spot in this whole awful situation."

"I can't believe that you actually *met* Randy Dean!" Bess exclaimed. "That's too awesome! What's he like?"

Nancy yawned. The morning sun was streaming through the window. "Really nice, Bess. He acts like a regular guy. But you'll have a chance to meet him," Nancy said. "He's staying right here in the hotel. And he invited us to come watch him making his TV special. I hope we can."

"What do you mean, you *hope* we can?" Bess demanded. "Wild horses couldn't stop me!"

Nancy smiled. "I don't know about wild horses, but we are here on an investigation, remember."

Bess stared at her, aghast, then immediately brightened. "Oh, we'll solve it in plenty of time," she proclaimed.

"Listen, Bess," Nancy said as she ran a brush through her hair. "I think the missing marmots are being shipped out tonight." She told her friend about the phone call. "I know you're not going to like this," she continued slowly, "but we need to move to the campsite to watch the situation more closely."

"Oh, no!" Bess wailed. "Leave the hotel just when Randy Dean arrives? And move into a cold tent? I'll die!"

"Oh, come on, where's your sense of adventure?" Nancy asked lightly. "Besides, if I'm right that tonight is *the* night, it won't be for long."

"Well—okay," Bess said gloomily. "I'll do it, but don't expect me to enjoy it."

"After breakfast I'm going to head over to the ranger station to talk to Martin Robbins. Maybe he can assign some rangers to patrol the campsite tonight. Ned also thought he might have a tent and a couple of sleeping bags we can borrow," Nancy said.

Bess dusted powder on her nose, then frowned at her image in the mirror. "What about me?" she asked.

"I want you to track down the Turkowers," Nancy said. "See if you can find out what they're up to today. I'll pick you up here when I come back from seeing Robbins, and we can go out to the campsite together."

As she walked toward her car, Nancy noticed a piece of paper tucked under the windshield wiper. It might be a circular of some sort, she thought, but she had a hunch it wasn't. Distinctly uneasy, she unfolded the paper.

The message was short and to the point: "Mind your own business, Nancy Drew. Marmots aren't the only things that can disappear!"

Chapter

Twelve

NANCY STARED at the note. It had been written in large, square letters with a red marker on a piece of computer paper. It resembled the paper they were using at the campsite, but she'd have to compare it to be sure. Still, with the key to the command post missing, that hardly narrowed things down.

She leaned against the side of the car and thought. The poachers were obviously desperate to get her off the case. They'd tried to put her out of commission twice the day before—and now this note. She'd planned to watch her main suspects closely, but it made her uneasy to think that they had their eyes on her, too.

Nancy put the threatening note in her pocket, got into the car, and started for the ranger station. As she drove, she found herself frequently checking the rearview mirror, but she didn't see any sign that she was being followed.

When she entered Martin Robbins's office, he was standing at the big wall map of Yellowstone with a sheaf of papers in his hand. He turned and said, "Hello, Nancy. What brings you here?"

"I wanted to fill you in on what's been happening with the case," she said, joining him at the map.

As she recited everything, beginning with the incident at the falls and ending with the conversation she'd overheard between Trainey and Gerald Turkower, Martin's frown deepened. "You've been busy. And it looks like you're making progress flushing these characters out." He crossed his arms and said slowly, "But from what you say, you've haven't got enough proof for me to move on." He went behind his desk and sat down, then gestured toward a chair.

"I know that," Nancy said, sitting down. "That's why I'm moving to the Emerson campsite today. From what Trainey said on the phone, I think the missing marmots are going to be shipped out tonight, and I'm pretty sure they're being kept someplace nearby," she replied.

The ranger nodded. He remained silent for a moment, then hit the desk with his fist. "I feel as if my hands are tied on this. Without more proof, I can't justify a full-scale search of the area around the camp, but I will beef up the patrol vehicles along that stretch of the highway tonight."

Nancy smiled slightly. "That will help. And that reminds me—there's something else you can do for me. I was wondering if you have some camping gear I could borrow. All my friend Bess and I really need is a tent and two sleeping bags."

Robbins chuckled. "And a couple of air mattresses, too, believe me. Otherwise, you'll be so sore after one night that you won't be able to walk. Let me think. I know I have a couple of sleeping bags here, but I may have to call around to get you a tent. And anyway, I'm not sure it's such a great idea. These people have already shown how ruthless they are."

"I know that," Nancy replied grimly. "That's why I have to stop them now."

Robbins rubbed his chin thoughtfully. Finally he said, "Well, all right, but on one condition—you call me the second anything starts to go down. I don't want to take any chances."

"I understand," Nancy told him.

He made a call. "One of the rangers over at Tower Junction has a tent he can lend you. He'll be passing by here in half an hour, so he'll drop it off. Okay?"

"Great," Nancy replied. "Thanks a lot. I guess I'll go get Bess and drop her by the campsite, then come back."

She started to get up, then sank back down in her seat. "There's one more thing. You've got two park maintenance men named Richard and Piker. I saw them talking to the Turkowers. That's just one of the things that makes me suspicious of them. How well do you know them?"

Martin leaned back in his chair and gazed toward the ceiling. "If you mean personally, I hardly know them at all," he finally said. "As far as their work goes, no complaints about them."

Nancy looked at Martin earnestly. "I know this is slightly irregular, but could I please see their personnel files?"

Martin frowned. "I'm sorry, Nancy. Those files are confidential."

"Oh, of course, I understand," Nancy replied. "I wouldn't dream of asking you to do something that's against the rules. But you have the right to consult their files, don't you?"

"Of course I do," Martin said.

"And if you looked through them and noticed anything that might be important for me to know, it would be only natural to mention it, wouldn't it?"

A slow smile spread across his lips. "That's so," he said, getting up and crossing to a bank of gray metal file cabinets. He scanned the labels on the drawers, then opened one near the bottom and pulled out two olive-colored hanging file folders. "Here we are," he said. "Richard Geismar and Piker Slattery."

He opened the first of the files and glanced through it. Next he looked at the second one. "That's funny," he said. "These two guys both grew up in Ashland, Idaho. That's a little town about forty miles west of the park. They were born in the same year, too."

He flipped back and forth between the two files. "Odd," he continued. "Their job records are practically identical."

"Would you mind if I check one or two of their references?" Nancy asked. "I'd need to use your phone."

"I think that would be all right," Martin said. He grabbed a scratch pad and scribbled a couple of names and addresses on it, then passed it over. "Here are the most recent references."

Nancy dialed, but the first number Martin gave her was disconnected. She tried the next one.

"Hopper and Wade Construction," a polite voice said. "May I help you?"

Nancy put on her most professional voice. "I hope so. I'm calling from the National Park Service in Yellowstone." She gave Martin an apologetic look, but he just grinned. She turned her attention back to the phone, telling the woman that Richard and Piker were looking for jobs and had listed Hopper and Wade as a reference.

"Gee, I'm sorry, but I don't recognize the names," the woman said. "Just a minute, let me punch them into our computer." Nancy held her breath as the woman put her on hold. Finally, she heard a click over the line. "I'm sorry, but we don't have a record of anyone with either of those names. Are you sure you have the right company?"

"Yes," Nancy replied. "Well, thanks very much." She hung up. "Richard and Piker lied on their applications," she told Martin.

"That's enough to get them fired. It's strange —we usually check references," Martin said. "But it doesn't prove that they're poachers—

only liars. Come on, I'll get those sleeping bags and air mattresses for you."

They loaded the gear into the trunk, then Martin said, "I'll see you later," and went back inside.

At the hotel Nancy found Bess sitting in the lobby, wearing a blue workshirt and well-cut blue denim overalls. "I'm all ready to go camping," she announced. "At least, as ready as I'll ever be."

"What's with the Turkowers?"

"The desk clerk told me they went off for a day-long hike through the Grand Canyon of the Yellowstone," Bess replied dutifully.

"I wonder if that's where they really are," Nancy said, then explained that she'd gotten mattresses and sleeping bags from Martin but had to go back for the tent. "I'll drop you off at the campsite first," she went on a little tensely. "I want you to keep track of the professor."

Fifteen minutes later Nancy watched Bess trudge up the path to the campsite, two sleeping bags slung over her shoulder and a suitcase in her left hand.

Back at the ranger station, Nancy found a very grim Martin Robbins. "I checked out the other references those clowns gave," he reported. "Every one of them a fake. They're out of here first thing Monday morning whether you turn up anything against them or not. My next job will be to find out how they got through the hiring process in the first place. The system is supposed to prevent this kind of thing."

"This place is deserted," Bess told Nancy back at the campsite. "Everyone went off to the feeding stations to pack up."

"What about Trainey?" Nancy asked.

"That's the weird thing," Bess replied. "I went up to the command post a while ago and noticed the professor riffling through a stack of photos. When he got to one of them, he got livid. I mean, his face turned bright red and he stalked off to his tent, then hopped into a Jeep and blew out of here." She stared at her friend. "What do you think it means?"

"I have no idea," Nancy replied.

"Jack acted strange, too," Bess continued, frowning. "I asked him to help me feed Spike, but he brushed me off. I don't understand it. Just last night he was saying he could get really serious about me and today you'd think *I* had the plague."

"I don't know quite how to say this," Nancy said slowly, "but Jack has been more or less flirting with me, too."

"Really?" Bess's eyes grew round with surprise.

Nancy nodded.

Bess was silent for a long time. Tears welled up in her eyes, but she shook her head and angrily wiped them away. Finally she said, "You must think I'm a real idiot, falling for such a total phony. He was faking his interest in me the whole time, wasn't he?"

Nancy shook her head. "He's very convincing," she said. "And maybe he *is* sincere in a way. He may be one of those guys who doesn't feel good about himself unless he's got somebody falling in love with him. So he convinces himself that the lines he's passing out are true."

Bess straightened up, then put on a smile. "Believe me, from now on I'm staying away from him."

"Come on, Bess," Nancy said to change the subject. "This is the perfect opportunity to search Trainey's tent."

Bess became alarmed. "But he might come back at any time!"

"You can stand outside and keep watch."

"Well—okay," Bess said reluctantly.

The two girls walked across the campground that was half packed already. Nancy looked at the piles of boxes with a feeling of urgency. She had to get to the bottom of things before time ran out.

While Bess stood guard in front of Trainey's tent, Nancy slipped inside. There was a sleeping bag spread out atop an army cot, a single, well-worn suitcase, and a folding table with a laptop computer. Nancy knelt down and opened the suitcase, but all it contained were clean, neatly folded clothes. She turned her attention to a few papers next to the computer, which turned out to be notes for a report on the project.

Trainey's green coat and floppy green hat were lying on the cot. Nancy picked them up and felt through the coat pockets. In the inside pocket was an envelope that contained a single photograph. It was too dark to make it out. She put the coat and hat back the way they had been and hurried outside.

"What is it?" Bess demanded. "Did you find something?"

"Yes, this picture." In the bright sunshine, it was easy to distinguish the figure of a person in a green coat and green hat walking out of the hut by feeding station 1. The hat and coat were Trainey's!

Bess flashed her friend a puzzled look. "What's so important about this picture?"

Nancy pointed. "Look at the date and time at the bottom."

Bess read, then counted on her fingers. "Nancy!" she exclaimed. "That was just before the propane stove exploded. That proves it! Trainey caused Brad's accident!"

Chapter

Thirteen

THIS PICTURE IS proof, Nancy," Bess repeated. "Trainey had to have tampered with the stove."

"I'm not positive, Bess," Nancy said. "The picture's too blurry. It could be anybody wearing that hat and coat, and if it is Trainey, why would he keep such an incriminating picture? Why not destroy it?"

Bess gave the photograph back to Nancy. "I don't know."

"And besides," Nancy continued, "it seems likely that this is the picture that made Trainey so upset. What if this *isn't* Trainey? When he saw it, he must have realized that somebody was trying to frame him. He may even have figured out who."

Nancy scrutinized the photograph. The floppy hat and turned-up collar of the coat made an effective disguise. All that showed of the person's face was one cheek and part of the nose.

Frustrated, she was about to put the photo away when she noticed a small white spot on the person's nose. She studied it closely but couldn't tell what it was. It could just be a speck of dust on the lens of the enlarger.

She slipped the photo into her pocket just as she heard Ned, Jennifer, and Alicia come down the path from the feeding station.

"Welcome to Camp Marmotville," Alicia called.

"Thanks," Nancy replied. "How's it going?"

"We've got the packing under control," Jennifer said. "Hey, you haven't seen my dad, have you?"

"He left here in a Jeep about forty-five minutes ago," Bess reported.

Jennifer frowned. "Huh. He was supposed to meet us up the hill, but he never showed up. I think I'll check the other feeding stations. Maybe a problem came up." She walked off toward the road.

"Are those maintenance guys around today?" Nancy asked.

"I haven't seen them," Ned replied.

"What about Jack?" Nancy went on. "Is he still at the feeding station?"

"No. He came through about an hour ago but said he had paperwork to do," Ned explained. "I'm sure he'll show up in a little while."

"So you guys moved out here just in time for our big cookout," Alicia said, smiling.

"Cookout?" Bess asked with interest.

"Our farewell dinner," Alicia explained. "To celebrate the end of stage two of the study. I'm about to make potato salad. Anyone want to help?"

Bess gave Nancy an inquiring look, then said, "Sure, I'm game."

As they walked away, Nancy told Ned about Richard and Piker's references. "Can you get away? I want to check those guys out."

"Sure," Ned said. "I'll just take the time."

"I'm a little concerned about Professor Trainey now, Ned," Nancy said as she started the car and headed for the western entrance of the park.

She told Ned about the photograph she found in Trainey's tent. "What if I've been wrong about him? If he knew who was in that photo and went to confront him, he could be in danger."

"Do you think we should go back and look for him?" Ned asked.

Nancy shook her head. "Let's leave that to Jennifer for now."

The narrow road led down into a valley and across a railroad track into a town. She turned onto the main street. It was lined with two-story wood frame buildings and resembled the set for a western.

Just past the business district was a white building with a green slate roof. The sign out front identified it as the town hall. Nancy parked, and they walked in.

The Ashland Police Department occupied one big room on the ground floor. A husky man of about thirty was sitting at one of the two desks. The name plate on the desk said Chief Tucker. As Nancy and Ned approached the counter separating the waiting area from the office, he raised his head with a friendly smile. "Hi, folks, can I help you?"

Nancy introduced herself and Ned and explained that they were investigating a poaching scheme in Yellowstone Park. "You can call Chief Ranger Robbins to check us out," she added.

"Thanks, I'll do that." He swiveled to face the telephone and spoke for a couple of minutes, then turned back to them. "Well, now, Nancy and Ned, what can I do for you?"

"We need information about two men named Richard Geismar and Piker Slattery," Nancy said. "According to their files, they grew up in Ashland."

Tucker frowned. "Those names don't ring a bell, but I've only been here three years." He went over to the file cabinets along the back wall. "We've got files here that go back pretty far," he remarked as he flipped through one of the drawers. "If either of these guys were ever involved in anything illegal, it should show in this drawer. Ah, here we go."

He returned to his desk with two manila folders and began to leaf through them. "Well, well," he said. "Definitely not model citizens. Vandalism, grand theft auto, breaking and entering, arson. They did time for that one."

"Wow," Ned said. "It looks like you were right to suspect them, Nancy."

Tucker showed her a photo of a much younger Piker. "That's one of them," she confirmed.

"You watch your step with these fellows," Tucker said. "You know who could tell you all about them? Margery Milliken, the principal at the consolidated high school before she retired. Go down to the end of the street and turn right," he said, gesturing. "It's a white house. I'll call to tell her you're coming."

Nancy thanked Tucker for his help, and she and Ned returned to the car. They found the house easily. The woman waiting on the porch steps was wearing a dark skirt and a white blouse. Her gray hair was twisted up in a french roll. A pair of reading glasses dangled from her neck.

"Ms. Drew, Mr. Nickerson? I'm Margery Milliken. I understand you want some information about two of my former students. Come in."

She motioned them to the sofa. "Now, what do you want to know about Richard and Piker?"

"Whatever you can tell us," Nancy replied.

The woman tightened her lips, then shook her head sadly. "Not among my successes, I'm afraid. They both had bad records in school. But I think they might have straightened out if it hadn't been for Jeff Barnes. He was a year younger than they, but there was no question who was the ringleader, especially at the end."

"What happened?" Ned asked.

Ms. Milliken clicked her tongue. "One night the three of them stole a car. When it ran low on gas, they broke into a filling station about twenty miles west of here. To cover their tracks, they set the place on fire, but something went wrong. Jeff's hand was badly burned, and of course they were caught. Richard and Piker went to jail, but Jeff was still a juvenile, so he was given a suspended sentence. The Barnes family moved away right after that, and Richard and Piker have never shown their faces around here since.

"Thank you so much," Nancy said. They chatted a little while longer. Then Nancy and Ned told Ms. Milliken goodbye and returned to the car. Ned offered to drive.

Nancy was certain now that Richard and Piker were involved in the poaching, but they didn't sound like the organizers. Who then? If that Jeff Barnes were around, he'd be a perfect candidate.

By the time they got back to camp, the sun was low in the sky. Preparations for the cookout were in full swing.

"Ned?" Alicia asked. "Could you bring that big table from the shed? Jack said he'd do it this morning, but he never showed up."

"Sure," Ned said, and headed off.

"Is your father back?" Nancy asked Jennifer.

Jennifer was obviously worried. "No, and I can't understand it. Where can he be?"

Nancy wanted to say something reassuring, but she was worried herself.

When darkness fell, Nancy helped Ned build a fire while Bess set out plates, napkins, and bowls of cole slaw and potato salad. The hamburgers and franks tasted delicious, but Professor Trainey's absence spoiled the good time. People kept glancing over their shoulders into the surrounding darkness, then inching closer to the fire.

"Maybe Jack and the professor went off together and had car trouble," Alicia suggested.

Jennifer shook her head. "Jack has a two-way radio in his car," she pointed out. "All rangers do. He could have called the station and had somebody come by with a message."

Nancy's thoughts spun. What if her original idea, that Trainey was the head of the poachers, was right after all, and Jack had discovered it? Trainey and his gang might be holding Jack captive to keep him from interfering with the last phase of the operation.

As the party broke up, Nancy took Ned and Bess aside. "We have to take turns keeping watch tonight," she told them, checking her watch. "It's just eleven. I'll take the first two hours, then Ned can spell me."

Bess nodded and quickly ducked into the tent, leaving Nancy and Ned alone in the moonlight.

"Should I stay with you?" Ned asked. "It might be safer."

Nancy put her arms around his neck. "I'd love you to, but you might distract me from my job. Besides, you need to rest before your shift."

"All right. Be careful, Nan," Ned whispered. He gave her a lingering kiss, then went to his tent.

Nancy watched him go with a sense of regret and loneliness. She crossed the campground to the spot she had picked out earlier, next to a large lodgepole pine. It gave her a clear view of the campsite but kept her hidden in deep shadows.

The camp grew quiet. In the distance an owl hooted. Somewhere closer, an animal crept stealthily through the underbrush. Nancy shivered and pulled the zipper of her jacket up higher. Ghostly wisps of white fog began to drift by. Nancy shifted her position, folded her arms tight against her chest, and scanned the camp.

As the minutes ticked by, she felt her eyes closing. So she decided to walk around to keep from falling asleep. She circled the campground, then walked halfway down the road that led to the highway. Stopping just before the last bend, she saw a truck move by, its empty rear end rattling.

She tensed. It seemed odd to be traveling through the park at that hour. Without stopping to think, she raced down the road, reaching the highway just in time to see the truck turn into the woods about a quarter of a mile east. It looked to Nancy to be near the spot where Piker and Richard had been working on the new trail.

She jogged to the place where the truck had disappeared, realizing that there was a dirt access road there. The maintenance men had probably used it to move supplies into their work area.

Nancy turned in and kept running. She'd covered about a half a mile when she saw the truck parked up ahead. She slowed and made her way up to it cautiously.

She heard a low voice on the far side of the cab. It was Richard! A flashlight clicked on, illuminating the figures of the two maintenance men.

"Hurry up," Piker said. "We've got a lot of work to do."

"Yeah," Richard replied. "I'm not looking forward to carrying all those cages."

Nancy's spine stiffened. That meant the marmots had to be stashed someplace nearby.

The two men began moving forward. Nancy followed at a safe distance. The access road ended about twenty feet beyond the truck, dwindling into a path that wound up a hillside.

Her calf muscles were feeling the strain of the climb, and she began to notice that the trees were thinning out. Nancy spied a cabin to the right of the trail. Piker unlocked the door and the two of them went inside.

Nancy circled the cabin and saw a small window in the back. She crept up to it, pulled herself up, and peered in through the dusty pane.

Her breath caught in her throat. Lining the walls were dozens of cages of marmots. Nancy could hear Piker. "That tranquilizer is strong. They'll be under for a few hours, plenty of time to get them all into the truck and out of here."

"How much longer do we have to hang around here?" Richard asked.

Piker shrugged. "Until the boss gets back.

He said he wanted to nose around the camp to make sure the kiddies were all in bed."

Nancy let herself down from the window. Any minute the boss could come back. She had to get out of sight. She was turning to go when two strong hands grabbed her and forced her arms up behind her back!

Chapter

Fourteen

NANCY'S CAPTOR HUSTLED her around to the front of the cabin, kicked the door open, and shoved her through. She stumbled into the light and fell to the floor. Piker and Richard spun around, startled.

"We've got a visitor," a familiar voice announced.

Nancy looked up. Jack Billings was standing next to the open door, a revolver in his hand pointed toward her.

She sat up cautiously as he approached. The gun was about two feet from her face when she noticed the burn scar on his hand.

Just then everything fell into place.

"Hello, Jeff," she said as calmly as she could. "Didn't anyone ever tell you that keeping the same initials when you take an alias is one of the oldest mistakes in the book?"

"You *have* been doing some investigating, haven't you?" he said.

Nancy swallowed. She desperately needed to play for time. If she could stall the three of them, Ned might come searching for her or one of the patrol cars Martin Robbins had assigned to the area might check up the access road.

"Your poaching plan was pretty clever," she told Jack. "How did you come up with it?"

Jack leaned back against the doorjamb but kept the gun pointed at Nancy. "I saw an article a while back about Randy Dean and his marmots. It said that people were paying a lot of money for them."

Nancy nodded, and he continued, apparently glad to have an appreciative audience. "A little later I was sorting the mail at the ranger station when I came across a letter from Trainey about the marmot study. I saw my chance right away and volunteered to serve as liaison to the project."

"And you managed to get Richard and Piker hired as maintenance men in spite of their forged references," Nancy guessed.

"You hear that, guys?" Jack said mockingly. "She's onto you."

"Come on, enough chitchat," Richard said. "Let's pack up and get out of here."

Anger flashed across Jack's handsome face. "I'm the one who makes the decisions around here," he growled. "Get those cages into the truck. I'll make our guest comfortable."

While Piker and Richard started carrying cages out of the cabin, he took some rope and tied Nancy's wrists behind her back, then tugged her toward a door in the corner of the room.

"Hey, Prof," he called, shoving it open, "here's some company for you."

Trainey was sitting on the floor of the small storeroom, his hands tied behind his back. His face was caked with dried blood from a gash on his forehead. "Are you all right?" she asked as Jack pushed her down beside him.

He nodded. "I'm sorry they got you, too," he said in a low voice.

"I'm sorry we got either of you," Jack cut in. "I don't like complications. I did my best to convince you to stay out of our way. But you wouldn't listen, so you have to pay the price."

Keep him talking, Nancy told herself. "How did you manage to steal so many marmots?" she asked.

"Easy!" Jack bragged. "I had Piker and Richard steal some cages, then I got a printout of the transmitter signals. I knew the counts were done in the afternoon, so we started trapping right after dark on Tuesday and worked all night. We hauled them up here and removed the transmitters long before the college crowd was even awake."

"You missed Spike," Nancy commented.

"Spike," Jack spat out. "That friend of yours is really something. She is cute, though, I've got to give her that."

Nancy wanted to punch him.

Just then Piker and Richard returned for more cages. As they gathered up a second load, Professor Trainey asked, "Why did you try to kill Brad?"

Jack scowled. "I didn't," he said, rubbing the scar on the back of his hand. "All I wanted to do was discourage him, so I rigged the stove."

"But you were giving a slide show during the time it was sabotaged," Nancy said.

Jack gave her a self-satisfied smile. "Hey, that's right. I guess I didn't do it after all!"

Nancy thought quickly. "Alicia used the stove to make hot chocolate at about six-thirty, and Brad came on duty at seven-thirty. So the stove had been rigged by then."

Jack leaned back against the door frame. "You're pretty good, Nancy. But you should have checked that out more. The narration for the show was taped. I started it, then slipped back to the campsite."

Nancy nodded.

"Borrowing the professor's coat and hat was a nice touch, you've got to admit," he went on. "If anyone saw me, they'd suspect it was him."

"Except for the fact that one of the time-lapse cameras caught you leaving the hut," Trainey said dryly. "The moment I saw it, I realized it was you who had tampered with the stove."

Nancy turned to Trainey. "How? I found the picture in your tent but couldn't tell who it was."

"I had an advantage over you, Nancy," Trainey explained. "I remembered that Jack had been bitten on the nose by a marmot and wore a bandage for a few days."

"The white spot!" Nancy gasped. "So that's what it was."

There was a loud crash outside, and Jack rushed out the door.

The moment he was out of sight, Nancy started struggling against her rope. Pain shot through her wrists, and she could tell she was getting nowhere. "How did he capture you?" she asked Professor Trainey.

"Sheer stupidity," he replied. "When I saw

that picture, I got mad and rushed off to find him. I met up with him at feeding station two, which is near here. He hit me, and when I came to I was in this cabin."

Jack returned with Piker. "Okay, let's go," he said, and grabbed Trainey by the front of his shirt and pulled him to his feet. Nancy managed to stand up on her own.

To distract Jack, she asked, "Were you the one who pushed me off the platform and tried to run me off the road?"

"Not guilty," he replied. "That was Richard. He knocked out your boyfriend, too. Ned walked in while Richard was stealing the tranquilizer."

"You're a real bunch of creeps," Trainey lashed out.

"Calm down, professor," Jack told him. "I gave you all plenty of warnings. I even put a note on Nancy's windshield. Why didn't you pay attention? It's all your own fault. Okay, Piker, grab that roll of tape and a flashlight."

"Where are you taking us?" Nancy asked as Jack shoved her and Trainey toward the door.

"I want to show you one of Yellowstone's natural wonders," he replied blandly, taking the pistol from his belt.

He and Piker forced them to march up the hill behind the cabin while Richard walked off toward the truck. The fog had thickened. Even with the flashlight, it was impossible to see more than a few yards ahead.

They reached the crest of the hill and started down. At the foot of it, Nancy stopped abruptly. Just ahead was a large crack in the earth, a dark, ominous ribbon snaking its way across the ground.

"What's that?" Nancy asked Trainey, trying to hide the fright she felt.

"It looks like a runoff fissure," Trainey said. "Every geyser has one. It's the path the heated water takes after being shot into the air. It comes down the side of the geyser cone, collects, and runs along the fissure to underground pools."

"Exactly, Professor," Jack said.

While Jack held the gun, Piker taped Nancy's ankles together, then picked her up and wedged her down into the fissure. Trainey was lowered next to her.

"Come on, Piker," Jack said. "We've got to finish loading the truck. Let's get out of here."

"Wait," Nancy cried, but there was no response. "Professor Trainey?" she asked. "What's going to happen?"

Trainey's voice was grave. "If I have my bearings right, the water from Princess Geyser takes this path down the hill." He stared at Nancy. "It erupts every two hours or so."

"You mean this fissure could fill up with boiling water soon?"

Trainey closed his eyes. "That's right."

A sudden hissing noise broke the silence.

Nancy gasped. It was the geyser! Any minute they'd be scalded to death!

Chapter

Fifteen

NANCY SHUT HER EYES and concentrated on rubbing the ropes on her wrist against a rough place on the fissure wall. Was it her imagination or could she feel one of them give just a bit?

Besides her, Trainey groaned.

She twisted her right arm, trying to get added leverage against the rope. She was sure that her skin was raw by now.

The hissing grew louder. Nancy saw the glitter of reflected moonlight on rushing water below where she was wedged. Damp steam rose and enveloped her. With a desperate yank, she managed to pull one hand out of the looped rope, then free the other. She let the rope fall.

"Listen, Professor, I've got my hands free. I'm going to try to climb out, then pull you to safety."

"Good luck," Trainey said.

Nancy noticed the rotten egg smell of sulphur. Her eyes were stinging. Cautiously, she brought her arms around in front of her and pressed her palms against the opposite wall of the fissure, then moved her knees up a couple of inches.

"We're running out of time," Trainey gasped. "The water is rising too quickly."

"I know." Nancy patiently worked her knees and hands upward. Her arm and leg muscles threatened to cramp, but at last one hand touched the top of the fissure. She grabbed hold, then quickly twisted, swinging her other hand to the other lip, just above where her head had been. Before her lower body could slide down into the crevice, she hoisted herself up. For a minute her feet dangled dangerously near the bubbling water at the bottom of the fissure.

Then she thrust herself onto the edge and rolled away. She took a deep breath, tore the tape off her ankles, then leaned over to unbind Trainey's hands and feet.

The professor was panting by the time she'd

talked him through the maneuvers that allowed him to climb out of the fissure.

"We got out just in time," Trainey said, once he'd caught his breath. He looked back at the crevice. The boiling current was halfway up the walls now. "Thanks to you, Nancy."

"We can talk later," Nancy said. "Right now, we've got to stop that shipment from going out."

Nancy raced up the hill with Trainey behind her. Reaching the crest, she abruptly skidded to a stop. "Can you make it back to the campsite?" she asked.

Trainey nodded.

"Good!" Nancy said. "Go get help. Martin Robbins or his men have to be around here somewhere."

"What about you?" Trainey asked.

"I'm going back to the cabin."

As the professor veered off in the direction of the campsite, Nancy crept down the hill toward the dark shape of the cabin.

She dashed to one side of it and crouched against the wall. Cautiously, she poked her head out. Richard and Piker were on the trail in front of the cabin, heading downhill toward the road. Both carried cages of marmots. Where was Jack?

Her pulse leapt as she heard footsteps behind her. Someone was coming! Nancy stood up and turned to find herself staring into Ned's eyes.

He threw his arms around her. "Nancy!" he whispered. "Are you all right?"

"I am now," she replied, returning his hug. "How did you find me?"

"I was in the woods and ran into the professor," Ned explained.

"We've got to stop that shipment from leaving," Nancy said urgently. She risked a quick peek in the window. Her heart sank. Only a few cages were still inside. There was no time to wait for reinforcements—they'd have to act alone. "Follow me to the truck," she whispered to Ned.

They crept quietly around the far side of it. "Now we wait," she told Ned.

In a few moments Richard and Piker came down the hill. "I'm glad that's over," Piker said.

The two men climbed into the back of the truck. Nancy and Ned raced up, slammed the doors shut, and pulled the metal latch into place. Richard and Pikcr began to shout and pound on the door, but there was nothing they could do. They were trapped.

Drawn by the noise, Jack came running down the path.

From the shadows at the edge of the trail, Ned launched himself toward Jack in a flying tackle. Taken by surprise, Jack crashed to the ground but recovered quickly and hit Ned in the face with his elbow. Ned recoiled, and Nancy saw Jack's fingers grope at his belt for his revolver. He was lifting it when Nancy raced over and aimed a karate kick at his wrist. Jack screamed and fell back.

"I'll hold him," Ned said breathlessly. "Find some rope or something."

Once Jack was tied up, Ned shoved him into the cab of the truck, then walked ahead, giving hand signals, while Nancy maneuvered the truck down the trail to the road.

As they drove up to the campsite, the truck's headlights lit up a crowd gathered near the firepit. Nancy recognized Bess, Trainey, Alicia, Jennifer, Martin Robbins, and, to her surprise, Edith and Gerald Turkower. Nancy hopped down from the cab as the others raced to the parking area.

"Nancy," Bess cried. "Are you all right?"

"I am now." Nancy smiled and hugged her friend. Then she turned to Martin. "Richard and Piker are locked up in the back."

"And here's the man behind the whole scheme," Ned said, triumphantly pulling Jack from the cab.

"Jack Billings? I can't believe it!" Martin exclaimed.

"What's a few marmots? The park's full of them, and I could use the money," Jack said.

Gerald stepped forward and, to Nancy's astonishment, produced a pair of handcuffs. "I'll handle him," he said.

"Edith and Gerry are agents of the U.S. Fish and Wildlife Department," Trainey remarked.

Bess looked startled. "What?"

"It's true." Gerald untied the rope and snapped the cuffs on Jack's wrists. "Dan called us in when the marmot traps began to disappear."

"Professor Trainey called you in?" Nancy repeated in surprise.

"Sure. We've been friends for years," Edith replied.

"That's why I didn't want you on the case, Nancy," Trainey explained. "I was afraid you might interfere with their investigation. Besides, look what happened to Brad when he tried investigating. I didn't want anyone else hurt."

Two park service cars pulled up next to the truck. Martin pushed Jack toward them. "I'll get this bunch into the cruisers."

Nancy turned to Gerald and Edith. "Your act sure fooled me," she said. "And when I overheard Professor Trainey calling you from the square dance, I was sure that he was the brains behind the poaching scheme."

Professor Trainey laughed. "That'll teach me to let my daughter drag me to dances," he said.

"I asked Dan to scout around for us today, but when we got back from Jackson a little while ago, we found out that he'd vanished."

"I'm afraid I was out of action," Trainey said, wryly. "Fortunately, Nancy was on the job."

Edith smiled. "Great detective work, Nancy! Did you know that there's a five thousand dollar reward for catching poachers?"

"Wow," Nancy said.

"Better start thinking about what to do with it," Edith went on.

The next morning Nancy was awakened by voices outside her tent. Bess was gone, so Nancy knew it had to be fairly late. She got up, threw on jeans and a sweatshirt, combed her hair, then stepped out into the sunshine. The sight that met her made her gape.

Two large trucks were parked near the campsite. From one of them came the rumble of a powerful electrical generator. Dozens of people were wheeling big blue metal equipment cases, rolls of cable, and light stands up the path to feeding station 1.

"Nan! Do you realize what's happening?" Bess ran over to greet her friend. "Randy Dean's going to shoot his special right here! He'll be here any minute, and I'm going to meet him if I have to sprain my ankle to do it!"

Nancy looked around. "Where is everyone else?"

"They're all up at the feeding station," Bess explained. "Come on, hurry!"

At that moment Nancy heard the low throaty growl of a perfectly tuned racing engine. She looked over her shoulder and saw a bright red sports car pulling to a stop in the lot.

"Bess," she said, "your prayers are about to be answered."

Bess gasped as Randy Dean stepped out of his car. "Hey, Nancy!" he called. "Good to see you again."

"Hi, Randy," Nancy replied when the rock star joined them. "I want you to meet my friend Bess Marvin."

Randy held out his hand. "Hi, Bess."

Bess turned pale, then red, as she took his hand. Still holding it, she gasped out, "This is just so totally awesome! I think you're the best singer ever!"

"Well, thanks," Randy replied. He gently

disengaged his hand and glanced up the hill. "Is that the way to the feeding station?"

Bess nodded.

"I'd better get up there. My producer will kill me if I'm late. Want to come?"

Bess just about tripped over her own feet as she moved to Randy's side.

At the top of the hill, Randy sat down on a folding chair while a makeup artist went to work on him. Dan Trainey was inside the enclosure, holding a marmot. The Turkowers, Ned, and the rest of the Emerson students were off to one side, watching. To Nancy's delight, Brad was among them.

"Hi." He grinned when she and Bess went over. "I finally talked them into letting me out of that place."

Nancy smiled and returned his greeting.

"Ned's told me everything," Brad went on. "Imagine, Jack being the mastermind of the whole scheme."

Ned kissed Nancy and then put his arm around her shoulders. "Didn't I tell you she was a first-rate detective?"

Trainey brought Spike over and handed him to Bess. He had removed the bandage. "This little fellow's ready to be set free," he said.

A stricken look appeared on Bess's face. "So soon?"

"It's time," Trainey said firmly.

"Oh." Bess turned away from her friends. Nancy could see she was fighting back tears.

"We have to do it, Bess," she said softly. "He belongs in the wild."

Randy joined the group. "I have a great idea," he said to Bess. "Why don't you release your little marmot as part of my show?"

Bess's eyes widened. "Me? On television?"

Randy nodded. "We'll release him together. It'll be a great sequence."

Bess was too stunned to speak. Then she looked down at herself and shrieked. "I've got to change my clothes!"

Nancy laughed as Bess placed Spike in his cage, turned, and ran down the hill to their tent. "I don't think I've ever seen Bess move that quickly," she said.

"Thanks for everything you've done, Nancy," Trainey said. "You've helped make this study a success and saved my reputation."

"You're welcome," Nancy replied. "What about the last stage of the project?"

Trainey sighed. "That part's not as successful. We can retag the marmots you recovered, but unless we can raise more money, the study ends right now."

Nancy smiled. "Would five thousand dollars help?" she asked.

Trainey stared at her.

"I'm donating my reward money to the project," Nancy explained.

"That's very generous, Nancy," Trainey replied. "Are you sure?"

"Yes, Professor, I know you'll put it to good use."

Ned put his arm around Nancy's shoulders. "Thanks, Nan."

"Say," Alicia said with a broad smile. "Maybe you and Bess could come back in August and help us with the last phase of the study."

"I'd love to," Nancy said, "but I don't know if I'm brave enough."

"Why?" Alicia asked. "Are you afraid of bears?"

Nancy shook her head. "No. I'd be too afraid to tell Bess that she has to camp out!"

Nancy's next case:

Nancy has come to Tokyo to attend the traditional Japanese wedding of a former exchange student, her friend Midori Kato. But the joyous occasion suddenly takes a dark and disturbing turn. For on the very day of the ceremony, the guests—anxiously awaiting Midori's arrival—are greeted instead by a shocking announcement: the bride has disappeared!

Did Midori have a simple change of heart or is there a more complex—and criminal—explanation? The answer comes to Nancy served on a silver platter: a near-fatal meal of poisonous fish intended to keep her from the truth. But with Midori's life at stake, Nancy refuses to back down and is soon drawn into a tightening web of jealousy, scandal, and deadly intrigue . . . in *The Runaway Bride,* Case #96 in The Nancy Drew Files™.

THE HARDY BOYS® CASE FILES